Moon Tribe: Revelation

Book One
The Moon Tribe Series

Sam Dei Lune

Moon Tribe: Revelation

ISBN: 978-0-165-47717-6

Chapter One

I wasn't looking forward to a girl's night out, not really at all, but my mother insisted that I spend some time with kids my own age, so I reluctantly agreed. At least tonight they had something different planned, something slightly more interesting than watching chick flicks and gushing about boys. Izzy and Tina were coming to pick me up in twenty minutes and I was still laying in my bed reading. *Shoot, I have to get dressed!*

I jumped out of bed and gave myself a quick look in the mirror. *Not good.* With a glance at my hair, I made the executive decision that a ponytail would be the simplest solution to my lifeless, long, straight, black hair. I rummaged through my closet looking for something remotely attractive to wear when I settled on my favorite black tank top. I was sure that I would be severely under dressed compared to the rest of the girls, but I knew that making it through the evening would be better done comfortably.

I've never been that great with makeup, but I know that if I show up with a bare face tonight I will stand out even more than usual. I glided on a touch of black eye liner and topped off my lashes with some mascara, then pouted my lips and smeared on some barely noticeable lip-gloss. Done with time to spare. I lay back down and picked my book up.

I can't wait until tonight is over so I can get home and back to reading, I thought to myself.

"Danni! Danni, your friends are here!" my mom yelled from downstairs. *Great. Here we go.*

"Coming!" I shouted back half-heartedly, as I rose to meet Izzy and Tina. I realized that it must have been a while since I last spoke because my voice was a tad horse.

Izzy and Tina were both really great. Izzy was the best friend I had and Tina was always so sweet, I really didn't ever have anything bad to say or think about either of them. It was just the whole dynamic of a girl's night that turned me off. I am often given grief by the other girls for being sick all the time, so being healthy on one of their big nights, I knew I would be endlessly guilted if I denied accompanying them while I was feeling well enough to do so. *Maybe it'll be*

fun. Maybe I won't feel like an outsider, I
thought. *Maybe, but not likely.*

"Hey guys, you look so pretty!" I greeted
the two fashionistas. They really did. Izzy
was always one of the prettiest girls
regardless of where she was. She was tall and
slender with short blonde hair and piercing
blue eyes. She could easily be mistaken for a
model, but as soon as she spoke, you knew that
she was only a girly girl on the outside. We
called her Izzy-Bee sometimes because she was
very busy, with boys mostly. She always dressed
up from her leopard print high healed pumps to
her dangly, glittering earrings.

Tina was really lovely too. She had dark
hair, like mine, but hers was shorter and
always had a healthy bounce. Like Izzy, Tina
was also tall and slender and always dressed
like she was ready to hit up a trendy
nightclub, even though we were not old enough
to get into any.

4

Izzy and Tina became friends while working together at the local coffee shop. They moved in together last week, shortly after our high school graduations. Izzy would be starting classes in the fall at a local college and Tina would be starting a job at an event-planning firm near by.

They seemed so at ease with their decisions and I envied that. I was enrolled to start a local private university, but was not excited and definitely not sure what I was going to be doing there. My school required me to live on campus so there was not much of an option for me to chose who I would live with or where I would be living.

"It's all a part of the college experience," my mom would tell me. This was a part of the experience that I was ready to do without. In the meanwhile, I was stuck living at home for the next two months until school started so I decided to make the best of it by burying my head in books until it was time for me to once again bury my head in required reading rather than the fiction novels I preferred.

"See you later mom" I kissed her on the cheek and hurried through the back door before she had a chance to give me a look over and criticize what I had decided to wear or how my hair looked. She meant well, but sometimes it was too much to deal with.

Tonight, I didn't want to deal with anything I didn't have to. I didn't wait to discuss who would drive, as I knew that even though we were meeting at my house, as mine was the only vehicle big enough to fit us all once we picked up the rest of the girls.

I popped open the trunk of my black Tahoe and pulled up the two third row seats so that I wouldn't have to get out of the car at a later stop when the regular seating in the car had been filled. Izzy jumped into her regular position in the front seat and Tina right behind her.

"Okay, just tell me where to go." I told Izzy. Even though this was a girl's night out, most of the girls were only friends through Izzy so she was the one that knew who was coming and where they would be.

Izzy gave me directions to each house and we picked up the remaining four girls, Anna, Nikki, Heather, and Alli.

"Where's this place again?" I asked Izzy once the last girl, Alli, was in the car.

"Uptown!" she spoke excitedly. I knew that she was looking forward to the evening ahead. We were going to have our fortunes read by a tarot card reader and then we would be going to a trendy Asian restaurant for dinner. I gave Izzy a half smile, not feeling enough excitement to give her a whole one, and turned onto the highway.

The streets were alive, as they always were in Uptown Minneapolis, Minnesota. I found a parking lot with available space that was almost in the middle of the two places we would be going, each within only a couple of blocks.

Walking down the street, we sounded like a group of horses with all of our healed shoes clicking and clacking on the cement sidewalk. I was always aware at the absurd amount of noise our shoes made when we traveled in groups, and it made me self conscious. Seemingly, I was the only one that felt this way because the rest of the girls trotted on confidently.

Minnesota was always hot and muggy in the summer. The humidity so thick at times that it felt like you could reach into the air and ring out water from nothing. Naturally, I was the only one there with a jacket on. The rest of the girls wore glittery and lacey barely there tank tops, which drew a lot of attention from the men we walked by. It didn't help that the girls were especially rambunctious this evening, giggling and squealing loudly all the way to the fortuneteller's store front.

I was the first to reach the door and as I opened it, I allowed the rest of the girls in ahead of me. They were much more excited about this than I was. I wasn't sure how I felt about having my tarot cards read. I didn't really think that I believed in fortune telling or any other superstitions, but I wasn't quit sure that I didn't either. Izzy walked up to the counter and spoke to the woman quietly.

She then turned around and said, "Who's first?" The woman reached for her arm and peered at me while she said something in a whisper to Izzy.

"Great! Danni, it's your turn."

"Oh, no, someone else can go first." I protested. I didn't want to be here nearly as bad as the other girls. They all wanted to know about their love lives and such but I didn't even know what there was in my life that was interesting enough to have my cards read.

"Come on, Danni." Izzy was now instructing me. Obediently, I walked up to the counter and followed the woman to the back room while I glared at Izzy for making me the guinea pig of the group. She gave me a big smile the way she always did when she was making me do something I didn't want to.

"My name is Maria", the fortuneteller said as she pulled out a chair for me, "Please have a seat".

I sat down quickly and reached my hand out to shake hers "Danni, nice to meet you" I was saying as she grabbed my hand and instead of shaking it she cupped my hand between both of hers.

"Interesting," Maria said under her breath, to herself, as she held on to me. She dropped my hand and smiled. "I knew there was a reason I was pulled to read you first, but I didn't know it was this strong," she acknowledged me.

I felt a shiver down my back, but I wasn't cold at all. In fact, it was pretty hot in Maria's back room. *Maybe I do believe a little bit, but what is she talking about?*

Maria shuffled her deck still smiling and began pulling the cards out one by one placing them in a formation on the card table in front of us. I noticed for the first time what a lovely woman Maria was. I was half expecting her to look bizarre and dress like a witch, but her appearance was quite normal. I would even say that she looked rather classy, with her silky black shirt, black dress pants, and fingers adorned with expensive rings.

My reading began, "You have a big change ahead of you. You are a spiritual person, but sometimes do or think things that go against your immediate beliefs of right and wrong; this is something that you will change as you learn about life and experience self-discovery as you grow. You have a deep passion in you for something that you have not yet discovered. You live in a fantasy world. Now, draw three cards and concentrate." I did as she told me, not really sure what I should be concentrating on. "You have a great love on the horizon. He is a generous man who will try very much to make you happy."

That was it? That was what all the fuss was about? I would finally be getting a love life and what, a change? I already knew that with college starting soon there would be a change and I was sure the rest was all a bunch of bologna.

I stood up and thanked Maria as I took out the money to pay her. She touched my arm with her other hand as she took the money.

"Be careful."

Why was she telling me to be careful when she just told me nothing but good things?

Crazy. That's it. Izzy has really done it this time. I just paid this lady to show me that she's nuts. I wasn't sure what I expected it to be anyways, but this was a bit far fetched even for my imagination.

"How was it?" Izzy asked when I walked into the reception area where the rest of the girls waited. They all looked up at me awaiting my answer and Maria was back at the front desk getting ready for her next victim.

"Fine." I said not wanting to ruin the night for the rest of the girls and so as not to hurt Maria's feelings.

"Great, me next!" Izzy jumped up and skipped to the counter. Maria smiled and politely took her back. I waited in the reception area with the rest of the girls thumbing through a magazine from the coffee table while the others gabbed to each other.

"Anything interesting?" Tina asked.

"Just some organizing tips" I answered. Tina looked at me confused for a moment, and then I realized what she was asking. "Oh, the cards, right. I guess I have a love on the horizon." Her face lit up. That was exactly what she wanted to know. That's what they all wanted to know… if their boyfriends love them or if they will find someone who will love them more, that sort of thing. I smiled at Tina and looked back down at the magazine, relieved to have some distracting unrelated reading material in the waiting room.

I was glad to get out of the storefront when the last of our group was done with having their fortunes told. The smell of fresh air seemed such a stark contrast to the scent of mixed incense that lingered in Maria's shop, even if the fresh air was somewhat thick, city air.

Walking to the restaurant was even more of an ordeal than walking to the fortuneteller's shop. The girls were feistier than before and more excited than ever to get into a closer vicinity to some hot-blooded men.

We were right on time for our reservations and were guided down a large staircase in the back of the main level of the restaurant. It led to a lower level seating area which was designed to seat larger parties. We were seated at a large round table beside a long rectangular table which was centered in the dining room, occupied by men who seemed to be just a few years older than us.

Many of the guys looked to be about the same age as us, but we knew that they were older because they had obviously been drinking alcohol, which we were too young to do at eighteen years old. The waitress came around and took our drink orders. Most of the girls ordered some versions of what are usually alcoholic drinks, but all virgin, of course, meaning all of the same ingredients except for the alcohol. Piña coladas, daiquiris and mixed juices were ordered by our table. I ordered a kiddy cocktail. I like the flavor and I really didn't care to look older than I was. Eighteen was just fine with me and I didn't think that I had a chance with any of the good looking guys at the table next to us even if I was of legal drinking age.

The table of men was getting louder and louder by the minute. We saw their waitress walk around the table and wrap a white piece of fabric around each of their heads, making them look like ninjas, and place a glass of beer, chop sticks, and a shot glass of sake in front of them. They each placed their chopsticks on top of their beer glasses about an inch apart and then carefully stacked their shot glasses on top of the sticks.

The moment the last shot glass was on the chopsticks the guys all shouted, "Bonsai!" and began pounding on their table causing the shot

glasses to fall into the beers. They quickly
lifted the large glasses and chugged the
contents down in large gulps.

The entire lower level of the restaurant
was looking and cheering at them. Our table
was the loudest. I glanced up at their table
to see if they noticed their newly acquired
cheerleaders and sure enough, they had. *Great.*
That was all I needed. Girl's night has now
turned into girls looking for boys night, as
usual.

I noticed one of the guys talking to the
waitress and pointing to our table. I was sure
I knew what was going on. He was going to ask
to buy us a round of drinks and she would have
to inform him that we were underage and that
would be the end of that. I was suddenly glad
that we were not able to drink. That would
definitely deter the group of excitable men.

I was wrong. The waitress came to our
table and told us that the young men at the

table next to us would like us to join them and
the staff had already taken the liberty to add
onto their long table so that there would be
room for us. The girls were ecstatic.

Why didn't I at least try to do something
with my hair? I was more self conscience now
than I had been the rest of the night. I knew
that the rest of the girls would find seats as
close to the guys as possible, so I didn't
worry about having to start conversation with
the males. I excused myself to the restroom so
that I would not have to be a part of the
scurry to seats next to the best looking guys.

I noticed the guy who had spoken to the
waitress about our table now talking to Izzy.
Of course, he had his eye on her since we
walked through the door; all he needed was an
excuse to get her attention. He jumped out of
his chair and moved to the end of his row of
friends so he could sit next to Izzy. Shoot, I
won't get to sit next to her now. Oh well,

maybe Tina will be closer to the end so that I can talk with her. No luck. She was sitting across the table from Izzy already engaged in a conversation with another one of the guys. I scurried to the restroom hoping that by the time I returned I would not have to think about where to sit because my spot would be chosen for me.

I didn't really need to use the restroom so I just stood in the mirror adjusting my hair and reapplying some lip gloss, trying to do the best with what I had. At least I wore some eye makeup. I always looked more put together when I had a little makeup on my eyes. By the time I estimated everyone would be seated I walked out of the restroom. I must not have been paying attention to where I was going because I walked right into what felt like a wall. Only, it wasn't a wall. It was a person.

He stood smirking at me.

"You okay?" he asked half laughing in a breezy tone. I was so embarrassed.

"I'm so sorry; I wasn't paying attention and… Are you okay?"

"I'm fine" he replied still smiling. I just stood staring at him, not sure what more to say when he turned and walked in front of me. Speechless for a brief moment, I stood frozen. He was gorgeous and I just made a fool of myself in front of him. *What else is new?* I thought.

I pulled myself back together and realized that I better get back to the table before they began to wonder if I had fallen into a toilet, that is, if they had even noticed that I was gone at all. I went into a full panic when I saw the table. There was no spot left for me at the end of the table where all of the girls were. They did forget about me! How embarrassing!

I shot a look to Izzy for support and she must have known what I was thinking because she shouted, "Your drink is down there, Danni, we saved you a seat".

I could have killed her. The seat they had "saved" me was the one that her admirer had left, leaving me pinned between two guys. That was not even the worst of it. The guy who was sitting immediately to my left was the very same man I had just plowed into on my way out of the restroom. The very same guy I had just made a fool of myself out of and was hoping I would never have to face again. Now, I would have to share a whole awkward meal right next to him.

Izzy gave me one of her smiles as if to say, "It's for your own good, live a little". I was infuriated with her, but I knew that she meant well. Any of the other girls would have been glad to be in my position, sitting between two gorgeous guys and obviously not by choice so as not to seem overtly desperate for attention. I sat down quietly trying not to look as uncomfortable as I felt.

The beautiful boy that I had plowed into just moments ago smiled over at me, "Hello again, did you miss me?" Great, he was going to tease me through this entire ordeal. I moaned uncomfortably and tried to smile back.

"Come on, it's not that bad, really. Do I smell or something?" he asked half joking. Actually he did. He smelled really good. He smelled like warm sugar and my mouth was beginning to water. What was wrong with me? Maybe I really do need a date if this guy is literally making me salivate.

After what felt like a full minute but realistically was seconds, I finally spit it out, "No. Uh, no, you don't smell and no, it's not that bad."

"Oh, good, you had me worried for a minute there." He laughed as if we had been friends for years.

He reached out and grabbed my hand to introduce himself to me "Charlie. And you are?"

"I'm Danni, nice to meet you, err, nice to meet you again, I mean." Just as I had finished, he leaned in and lightly kissed my cheek. That smell, what is it with this guy's smell? My mouth was watering again and my heart was beating at what felt like a million times a minute. Charlie pulled back slowly and laughed again. Did he have any idea what he was doing to me?

My dinner came and I pushed the food around with my fork for a little bit, making it look as convincible as possible that I was actually eating. When the waitress came around to check on us, I informed her that I was done and gave her my plate. She furrowed her eyebrows at my full plate, but took it away, to my relief, without making a comment. The food looked really good and everyone around me were enjoying their meals, but my stomach was doing flips and I was not interested in seeing what would happen if I actually put any food in it. The last thing I needed tonight was to vomit in front of everyone, to get sick in front of Charlie.

"Not hungry?" Charlie asked and then continued before I had a chance to say anything as if I had already given him the answer, "So, where are you guys headed after this? From the look of your friends, you must be going dancing."

I laughed, he was right about how they looked, "No, we're going home after dinner and they always look like they're going dancing. They're pretty aren't they?"

I don't know what caused me to ask him the last question but he didn't seem put off by it

and answered smoothly "Not my type, but yes, I
can see why you'd ask."

I didn't think that by saying my friends
were not his type that Charlie was implying I
was, but the implication that he was not
attracted to my friends relieved me a little
bit. My friends were Barbie dolls and I was
more of an action figure. Yes, most guys would
like to hang out with the action figures, but
they would much rather date the Barbie doll. I
was glad to meet a boy who didn't feel this
way, even if he didn't necessarily want to date
the action figure either.

After everyone's plates were cleared and
the bill came I glanced at Izzy giving her the
cue that I needed to get everyone home so that
I could get to bed. I was suddenly so worn
down I could think of nothing more than my
comfortable bed and going to sleep, well
nothing more than bed and the boy sitting next
to me. The thought of Charlie made me blush

and I was instantly grateful that it was too dark for anyone to notice.

When I noticed the guys pulling out their credit cards, I did the same, but the boy to my right grabbed my hand and told me to put it away.

"We get dinner tonight and you guys come to our party next week," he bribed. I looked to Izzy for a reply and could see that she had already agreed to these terms. I was really uncomfortable with having someone else pay for me, but I did not want to seem rude so I arbitrarily agreed to the suggested plans.

"Thanks," was all that I could get out; even though I knew that I was not really planning to go to any party with a group of strange boys any time soon. We all stood up to leave, a few of the guys and girls were exchanging phone numbers, Izzy and the guy she was speaking to all night were among those doing so.

Charlie stood to walk out and stopped suddenly, standing in front of me, "See you later, Danni," and kissed me again on the cheek.

"What was that!?" Izzy squealed in a loud, excited voice.

"Don't ask me" is all I could reply, much quieter than her question had been asked. I really didn't know why he kept kissing me, but I guessed it was because he enjoyed making me flustered.

The car ride home was even more charged than even the car ride to Uptown had been. Everyone was talking about who they met, what they discussed and how they exchanged numbers. The most important topic was, of course, next weekend's party that we were all apparently going to.

Izzy flashed the same smile she had already given me twice that night right before she had done something I would disapprove of and turned to everyone else in the car, "Danni met someone too, and I saw him give her a little smooch!"

"Izzy!" she was as bad as Charlie, I officially was doomed to spend my entire night embarrassed and uncomfortable. We dropped the rest of the girls off and Izzy, Tina and I drove back to my house. We all jumped out and gave our goodbye hugs.

Izzy and Tina walked to Izzy's car and I to my door when Izzy called out to me, "We're going shopping tomorrow, and I want you looking really sassy next weekend." I cringed and didn't respond. I knew that there was no point in arguing with her. It wouldn't have made a difference anyhow because she almost always got her way. Besides, I thought, it wouldn't hurt for me to get some new clothes regardless of the intended purpose. I could worry more specifically about what those clothes would be tomorrow.

I walked in to my house quietly hoping not to alert my mom to my arrival. I washed my face and got ready for bed. Climbing into bed felt even better than I thought it would. I pulled my covers over me and eyed my book. I had thought that I would want to read before bed as I do most nights, but tonight I was having a difficult time focusing my eyes and decided sleep is what I needed more than anything, well, maybe not anything.

Chapter Two

I woke up feeling refreshed. For the first time in a long time I had experienced a really deep sleep. I didn't remember what I had dreamt about, but I was sure that I had some kind of good dream because I woke up in a great mood. I grabbed a hair tie off of my nightstand and tied my hair up before I walked to the bathroom to brush my teeth and wash my face. By the time I walked downstairs to the kitchen my mom was already awake and drinking her coffee.

"Izzy called and said she would be here in an hour to pick you up." I looked at her for a couple of seconds confused. Then I remembered last night and that Izzy and I were going shopping today. Ugh, why didn't she call or text me instead of my house? Then I realized it was because if she told my mom that we had plans it would be more difficult for me to weasel my way out of them.

I grabbed a banana and turned back towards the stairs. That was when it hit me again, that smell. Mmmmmm… it's so good. The smell of warm sugar seemed to travel through my entire body and was heating up the blood in my veins. My pulse began to increase again, but this time I was able to control it and the blush left my cheeks right away. Actually, the blush left me cheeks the moment I realized what I had just smelled. I smell him. I smell him in my hallway. How is that possible? Was it just the memory of him that influenced this physical reaction? If so, why has the smell not gone away? I shook my head trying to release the scent from my nose but I couldn't shake hard enough, because the smell was still there. My mind was playing tricks on me. Was I really so enticed by this stranger that it was affecting me this much? Apparently this was so, because I had committed his scent to memory after just one night.

Maybe Izzy was right; I did need to get out more. At that, I remembered Izzy and the fact that she would be there to pick me up soon. I grabbed my usual attire, t-shirt, jeans, leather jacket, and threw them on my bed as I grabbed a towel and jumped into the shower.

I find that taking a shower is usually the most peaceful time of my day. It's the time that I take to think about things and to recoup. The beading of the hot water on my skin relaxed and invigorated me at the same time. There was no way that I would be able to take on my coming day without taking this time for myself. I let the water flood over my face as it met the back of my head, washing away the shampoo. The amount of time I took just standing and thinking in the shower far exceeded the time I took actually getting ready.

By the time I was dressed and ready to go Izzy was already at my house. She sat in the living room chatting with my mom about who knows what. The two of them could go on for days talking about what the latest trends were and local gossip. My mom was a lot like Izzy, they were both beautiful and they both seemed to draw people to them. Men reacted to my mom the same way they reacted to Izzy too.

My father passed away when I was little so I didn't have any memory of him, but from

what I had been told, he worshipped the ground
my mother walked on. It was always Dan and
Ella back then. That's where my name came
from, Daniella. I was supposed to be the
perfect mix of the two of them, but really, I
think I got the worse of each.

"Okay kids, break it up", I called down to
them. Izzy stood up and gave Ella a hug.

"See you later Ella, maybe next time Danni
will let us play longer", she said with a wink.

Ella gave me a kiss and slipped her credit
card into my hand against my will, "Go have
fun, Danni. Be a girl".

I hated it when she said that to me. Most
parents would be glad that their daughters
would rather stay home than go out on the town,
scantily dressed and hunting for boys, but not
my mom. She could not seem to understand what
was wrong with me, but she was convinced that
if I spent enough time with Izzy some of her
girlish charm would rub off on me.

What Ella didn't quite see about Izzy was that she put on a good front. Rather than chasing boys, Izzy would much rather be hunting down a larger prey, shotgun in hand. Izzy loved the outdoors and outdoor sports. Maybe hanging out with Izzy was the trick after all. Maybe she could show me how to seem glittery and shiny on the outside and still be able to roll in the mud at my own free will. Oh, but the glittery part seemed like so much work, the hair, the face, the clothes, the boys… there it was again, warm sugar. I must have spaced out a bit because Izzy had to ask if I was okay.

"Yea, just a little hungry I think." At least it was kind of true.

"We'll grab something when we get to the mall" Izzy replied, looking somewhat concerned.

The mall was chaotic. There were people everywhere and I was already feeling drained.

Izzy had a fire in her eyes as soon as she saw the stores, but then looked at me squinting a little, "Do you need to go eat right away?"

"No, we can shop, Izzy. Where do you want to start?" I asked her. She pepped back up and grabbed my hand. *Oh no, I was in her territory now.*

We went through three stores before we finally found one that I felt comfortable in. After circling the entire store, we each grabbed an armful of clothes and climbed into the dressing room area.

"You first", I told her as I sat on the cushy chair in the mirrored room. Izzy tried on the clothes, coming out of the dressing stall each time she wore a new outfit so that I could see her. Each outfit looked better than the last. She really had an eye for fashion and a way of putting together the most flattering ensembles.

"Why even bother, Izzy, you look good in everything," I said. She scrunched her nose at me and went to her dressing room to change back into the clothes she wore to the mall.

My turn on the impromptu runway didn't go as successfully as Izzy's. I hated the way each outfit looked on me and I was feeling defeated.

"Wait just a minute," Izzy said, "I saw something I think you would like. Izzy returned with a pair of jeans that looked a little beat up and a black tank top entirely made of lace. It wasn't too glittery or shiny, so I was satisfied thus far.

I thanked her, taking the garments and returning to what I was now referring to as the torture chamber. Calling it that did make her laugh a bit, but I could tell that she was getting annoyed by my indecision and was reaching her wits end.

I slid on the jeans, "The pants look pretty good, but they're a little long…" I slipped on the black lace top over a black tank top I already had on under the t-shirt I had been wearing, "It's nice, but maybe a bit revealing…"

"Oh shut up and get out here!" she finally shouted at me. Apparently she had finally reached the end of her rope and this made me smile.

"Now you know how I feel", I told her.

"Danni, yes, that's hot! I love it! You're getting it! The jeans will be just fine with heels, and I hate to break it to you kid, but you are wearing two tank tops, if that's revealing you need help I can't give you."

So, it was decided, not only was she making me get this outfit, but also a new pair of shoes.

"Something with a tall heel", she requested.

I agreed, but only if I could get a sweater, "You know, just in case I get cold", I lied.

After scuffing through more stores than I cared to count, I found a pair of black high heeled shoes and a black sweater for next weekend's charade.

I must have eased up on the idea of shopping a little bit because I even picked up a pair of red chopsticks for my hair. I was standing in line to pay for them while Izzy was looking at the necklaces when my new item caught her attention.

"What are you getting?" She asked very curiously.

"Just these", I answered nonchalantly. The biggest smile I had ever seen grew on her face like she was seeing Santa Clause for the first time.

"Seriously, are you really that happy that I'm accessorizing?" I asked her slightly irritated.

"No, Danni, look what you're accessorizing with. You have chopsticks on your mind", she replied accusingly.

I then realized what she was speaking of when the image of Charlie placing his chopsticks onto his glass the night before popped into my head.

"What? That's insane. I just thought that they would help with the whole hair situation! I am not thinking about *him*!" I wasn't even convincing myself. At the blatant thought of him, his scent was heating up my insides again. What was wrong with me?

I must have been looking flushed again because Izzy looked worried "We need to get some food in you, Danni."

"Maybe just a juice stand", I replied. I couldn't eat with my stomach doing flips like this again.

The line for the juice stand was long and moved very slowly, but this gave me plenty of time to decide what I wanted, which is good thing because I am usually pretty indecisive.

Izzy and I each got our drinks and were walking to find a bench to sit at when I suddenly felt a cold burning sensation in the palm of my hand. I dropped my shopping bags from the shock and looked down at my palm looking for what I thought was an enormous paper cut. There was nothing there.

"What's the matter, Danni? Do you need help carrying all two of your bags?" Izzy asked sarcastically, laughing at me. Tripping, dropping things, anything that makes me look stupid is pretty much the norm for me, so Izzy was not surprised at all that I would drop my bags. She, on the other hand was carrying six full bags with no problem at all.

"I think there's something up with my hand, it was kind of burning," I told her while still examining my hand to find out what caused the odd sensation. When I looked up at her she had an even bigger grin on her face than she did when she saw that I was purchasing chopsticks earlier that day.

"Honestly, Izzy, I'm not just making an excuse", I told her in a matter of fact sort of way.

"I didn't say you were; it's just that your timing is…" She didn't get to finish her sentence before I noticed someone was standing behind me holding my shopping bags.

"Did you get anything nice?" he asked with a half smirk on his face as he opened the top of one of my bags and peered in.

"I don't see how that's any of your business", I snapped at him.

"Nice to see you again, Danni", Charlie said in his smooth honey voice as he leaned in kissing my forehead this time. What was with this guy? He's known me for less than twenty-four hours and already he greets me as if we're best friends.

Then it happened again, the sweet warmth, and it was all over for me. There was no chance for me say anything to him about his behavior because I was too worried about the drool falling out of my mouth if I tried to open it.

I stood there like a statue while Charlie chatted up Izzy about how fun last night was and how his friend Nick, the one that sat next to and talked to Izzy all night, couldn't stop talking about her.

Charlie glanced at me with his devilish half smile every once and again, checking to see if I was still as heavily intoxicated as I was the moment before. Izzy finally looked over at me and noticed my pale face and red cheeks.

"Oh, you better sit down." She grabbed my arm and sat me onto an iron mall bench. "She's been like this all day, I wonder if she's coming down with something?"

"I wonder", he repeated, wearing a full smile this time.

"I'll go get you some water", Izzy offered as she walked away, not waiting for my answer. If she had waited for my answer, she would have known that the last thing that would make me feel better was being left here with Charlie, alone.

"How's your hand?" he asked, pulling it up from my lap.

"Fine", I finally let out, my first word in what felt like ages. He glanced up to see that Izzy was now waiting in line at a store to buy a bottle of water. She would be gone a while. Still holding my hand he traced his finger down my palm.

"You!" I jumped up from my seat. "How did you do that? You're the reason my hand... but how? What did you do to me?" Charlie rose from his seat very slowly still smiling at me.

"I knew you could feel me, Danni. I could tell when we met last night."

"Feel you? What are you talking about? Of course I can feel you, who wouldn't? What do you have under your nails, acid?"

He took a small step towards me and whispered into my ear, "Electricity." His whisper sent tingles down my spine, not because of the word he spoke, but because the instant he spoke it I was showered in that strange warmth, but this time it was too much.

Chapter Three

I woke up on a strange cot with what had to be a doctor flashing a light into my eyes and speaking to who must have been Izzy.

"What happened?" I mouthed as I tried to sit up.

"Slow down there; don't try to get up too quickly. You passed out. You're in the mall, the security office; I'm a doctor. Do you know you're name?" What the hell was he talking about? Of course I knew my name.

"Danni" I told him in an obviously annoyed voice. "Where's Izzy?"

"I'm right here Hun", she said sweetly.

"I'd like to go home now." I stated, not quite sure which one of them I should be speaking to. I heard the doctor asking Izzy who drove and telling her I should be taken to the hospital to make sure I don't have any injuries. The doctor stepped out of the room and Izzy kneeled down next to me.

"I just spoke with Ella and she's a mess. I don't want her driving like this. Charlie is going to take you to the hospital to make sure you are okay and I am going to pick up your mom so that she doesn't get into an accident or something."

"Charlie?" I asked, "What is he still doing here? I don't want to see him."

"That's not nice Danni. He's here because he's worried about you, and honestly, right now it really helps to have another person here.

I'm going to drop your bags at your home when I pick up Ella. Now, is there anything else that you need?" I shook my head no. "Then I should get going, and so should you. Don't give him a hard time, I'll see you soon". I felt like I was just scolded by my mother. The two of them had more in common than I thought.

Charlie came to my side and lifted me gently as soon as Izzy left.

"You okay? I didn't mean to scare you like that. It's just that I thought that you knew. You must, how could you not?" He looked genuinely confused as if I was the one that just threw *him* the curve ball. "Okay, Danni, we seriously need to talk. Are you really feeling alright or do you need to be seen."

"I'm fine!" I almost shouted, more emotionally than I thought it would come out.

"Call Izzy, tell her you're just hungry. Tell her I'm taking you to dinner. She'll be fine with that, trust me." I don't know why, but I listened to him. It went over much easier than I thought it would. Izzy and Ella were so happy that I was not only fine, but that I was going to dinner with a boy that they didn't even ask any more questions.

"Good, have fun, call me when you get home. I want all the juicy details", was all I got from Izzy.

Charlie and I walked out of the mall without exchanging any words. He opened the doors for me, walked silently beside me to his car, opened the car door for me and shut it once I sat down. After getting into the car himself, he looked at me and spoke slowly, "What are you thinking?"

"I need to know what you are talking about Charlie. I know there is something strange going on, but I can't even begin to guess what it is and I need to know, NOW."

He thought quietly for a moment and then replied, "Do you feel something when you are around me?"

What kind of question was that? And why was he answering my question with a question? I nodded my head and waited for his response. "We need to go somewhere." He threw his car into reverse and backed out of the parking spot. He had such an intense look on his face that I didn't want to disturb his thoughts to ask where he was taking me. Under normal circumstances I would never go to an undisclosed location with some strange man, but nothing about these circumstances were normal, so I just waited.

We pulled up to a large wooded lot that had a long spiraled driveway that looked much more like a street. You would never have known that this was not just another street to turn on if there hadn't been a sign at the entrance that read *Private road, no trespassing*. At the end of the winding driveway we reached a large stone house. The house was amazing and from one look at it I knew; this beautiful boy lived in this beautiful house. *Why am I here? Why would he take me to his house?* Charlie got out of the car and hurried to the passenger side to help me out of the car. He grabbed my hand and walked quickly to the door and let us in.

The foyer was grand and an enormous chandelier hung down from the second story. The décor was simple and elegant, muted colors and rich textures. The house felt as warm and exciting as he did.

After leading me to the living room he finally spoke his first words since leaving the mall parking lot, "Please, have a seat." Knowing that he was in no mood for arguments, I did as I was told. He began, "Now, Danni, I need you to be very specific here. It's very important that you tell me exactly what you feel when you are near me, and Danni, I need details."

From the ferocity in his eyes, I could tell that he was serious, but I still wasn't grasping what he was asking of me. I was so embarrassed that I could feel the crimson shade crawl up my neck and into my face like a shear red vale.

"Um, Charlie", I started, "This is really kind of personal to be asking of someone you have just met and I don't really think it's fair." He gave me a thoughtful look and raised an eyebrow.

"You're right. I'm sorry, my deepest apologies, Danni, but it really is important that you tell me and the sooner you do, the better."

"Fine," the sooner I got this over with the sooner I would be rid of this intrusive, stubborn, gorgeous man. "Well, I don't like that hand thing you do to me and telling me it's electricity is really infuriating, either you are expecting me to believe a little static energy would sting that much, you are implying that I am a wimp, or you are feeding me some extremely cheesy line, Charlie. It makes you seem like a real creep. But then there's that scent of yours. Expensive cologne, I'm sure, but I think that I am having some sort of allergic reaction to it because I smell it all the time and it makes me feel sort of faint. Finally, there's this kissing habit of yours, I know you must think that you are really something, but kissing my face every chance you get just to laugh at my reaction is really very cruel of you." The words came pouring out of my mouth like a confession waterfall.

Charlie looked like he had seen a ghost. He turned pale, looking as if all of the blood had been drained from his face. "What are you Danni?"

Another one of his dumb questions, this time I gave him the simplest answer I knew, "A girl."

I could tell that he wanted to be angry with me but couldn't be as his eyes stayed tense but a smile crawled across his face.

"You really don't know, do you?" The frustration finally got the better of me.

Tears were now running down my cheeks and I choked out, "Of course I don't know, Charlie! I don't even know what you're talking about or what kind of sick game you're playing, but here I am sitting in this strange place with this strange guy and I really can't take any more of this so please take me home!" I shouted at him as I stood and walked towards the door.

He looked confused, and then hurt, and then deep in thought. Then he smiled and asked me to take a seat again. *Oh no! He's a psychopath*, I thought. After all these years of being careful I walked right into the

secluded house of a psychopath! I sat down
immediately so as not to disturb him any more.
If I just react calmly, I might still have a
chance to live.

"I didn't mean to scare you, Danni, it's
just that I've never met anyone like you
before. Do you mind if I talk? All you have
to do is listen to me. Then, when I am
finished and you have heard everything I have
to say, you can leave if you want. Here." He
threw his car keys to me "You can even take my
car if you want."

I nodded my head silently, clutching the
keys so hard that I could feel them cutting
into my skin. I tried desperately not to lose
my cool again.

"So, Danni, it seems to me that you and I
are very similar in some unexpected ways. For
instance, this cologne you speak of does not
exist. That is me you smell and I would be
willing to bet that if you ask any one of your

friends they will tell you that they have no idea what you are talking about." He paused for a moment and asked, "What do I smell like to you, by the way?"

"Warm sugar", I muttered.

"Most guys wear cologne, this is kind of cologne for me, a sort of mind trick, if you will. My pheromones are charged to so that my scent is appealing to other people. This is not something that people normally even notice, but for you, it seems that my scent is very strong."

He waited for my response, but I gave none, so he continued, "Then there is this matter of my touch. My intention was to give you a little tingle of electricity, but somehow that was overly charged with you too, do you know what that means, Danni? I think that means you amplify my energy. I don't know how that is possible, but that's the only way I can explain it." At this point Charlie was getting more and more excited. He was pacing back and forth in front of me wildly and then stopped as if he had hit a brick wall.

"Danni, what are you?" This time when he asked he had real pain behind his eyes. I still didn't know what he was talking about but I knew that the answer that I gave last time would not suffice now. After all of his ranting, I was beginning to seriously question every notion I had about what was happening here too. He really believes that I am something other than just a girl. My heart was now bleeding for the pain he was in.

"I don't know", I cried.

"Danni, I am going to ask you a series of questions, if it seems that they apply to you, I need you to tell me. Can you do that?" I nodded. "Great. Thank you, Danni. This is really important to me, maybe to both of us." He said the last part so quiet I barely caught it.

He began his line of questioning and to each question I nodded. Insomnia? Yes. Sensitive to light? Yes. Frequent illness? Yes. Low blood iron? Yes. Vivid, colorful, lucid dreams? Yes. The questions went on and on and my answer to every one was yes. It was as if he knew more about my medical history than any doctor I have ever had.

"How?" I asked him.

"You're like me, Danni. I don't know how, but you are." He let out a big sigh and looked at me like he was about to tell me my dog died or something, "Danni, you are, well, you and I both are… Danni, you're a supreme being, a moon child." When he finally spit these words out I jumped out of my seat and bolted for the door. This guy is seriously delusional.

He stepped in front of me to stop me from running out and I shoved him with all of my might. I didn't expect this to deter him much as he was bigger and stronger than me, but he let out a loud yelp and when I looked to see what I had done, I saw my handprints burned through his shirt. *How did I do that?* I looked at his face for answers.

"It's my fault, I made you aware of your powers the second I told you what you are. He was so calm now when he spoke to me that it leveled me out too.

"It's okay, I'm not hurt", he replied to my unspoken question, "It only stings a little, but really, I'm okay. Promise." His perfectly sculpted abs were now showing through the burn wholes on his shirt. I looked away, flustered and embarrassed. Charlie must have caught my glance because he signaled for me to take a seat again and then turned towards the staircase.

"I'm going to go change my shirt, and when I get back, I'll explain everything."

While he was gone I started to take in the rest of the beauty the house had to offer, that

I was unable to notice before amidst all of the excitement and emotion. The floors throughout were cold grey concrete. The living room was furnished with a dark espresso brown leather L shaped couch that looked big enough to fit ten people. A massive sheep skin rug lay beneath a glass coffee table, which was covered in books and notebooks. For the first time since I met him, I wondered what Charlie did for a living. Maybe he was a student, but a student would not be able to afford this kind of home on their own, let alone most adults, and this did not look like an ordinary family house. It seemed to me that he lived here alone. The fireplace was covered in slate and what looked like an original art piece hung above it. My eyes traveled from one detail in this room to another as my curiosity about the rest of the house grew.

I made my way back to the couch where I was supposed to be sitting and waiting for

Charlie when I felt a cool breeze sweep through the room. Probably just a draft because of all the windows, I thought. I was thinking how cold it must get in this house during the harsh Minnesota winters when I saw Charlie walking back down the stairs. He walked into the living room and flicked on the light switch.

"So, you like sitting in the dark, do you?" he commented with a smirk on his lips. I hadn't even noticed it getting dark and wondered how long I had been there.

"Maybe you should call home and tell them that you and I are going to a movie after dinner so we can have more time."

"Good idea", I replied and pulled out my phone. Ella was as giddy about it as I thought she would be which made the phone call easy and quick.

While I made the phone call to my mom Charlie slipped into the kitchen and prepared a small meal of sautéed peppers and green beans.

I was grateful for this small gesture on several accounts. First, he had made it so I wasn't fully lying to my mother; we were at the very least having dinner. Second, I was starving, and while the dish was very delicious, anything would have been good at the moment. Lastly, I'd never had a guy cook for me before, and here was this gorgeous guy, way out of my league, cooking for me.

The dining room was fairly formal, but possessed the same amount of comfort as the rest of the living space. Charlie and I sat mostly in silence while we ate our impromptu meal. I say mostly because we both made "mmm…" sounds intermittently between bites.

When we were done eating we returned to the living room where I curled up on the couch. Charlie sat down next to me and tossed me a knotted throw, instinctually, knowing I was cold.

"Thank you", I almost whispered, trying to catch my breath after the warm sugar scent washed over me again through the breeze. *Stay focused, Danni. This is no time for swooning.* "So, tell me, Charlie, if I am a supreme being, why is it that I am so bitterly normal?" I was half expecting him to finally give up on the supreme being talk and tell me what was really going on when he started with his explanation to all of my inquiries.

"A supreme being is a human; we just are able to do things that other people cannot. Where do you think all of those alien and vampire stories come from? All of the ancient Greek myths, stories of magic and witches, those all came from us. The fact is, just because someone has a power or strength, does not mean that they know how to use it."

"But that's impossible, how would I not know my entire eighteen years of living that I am so different?" My words trailed off at the end, realizing that I had known I was different. I always knew I was different.

"I can teach you", He said, "I can teach you how to live better, how to use your powers, how to be what you were meant to be." He moved closer to me and took my hand, "I can teach you Danni, if you let me."

I looked into his eyes and knew that I could not deny him. This meant as much to him as it should have meant to me, to finally know my place in the world. Only, that wasn't the reason I decided to let him. I only wanted more time with him now. I only wanted to be near Charlie. I nodded my head and he smiled, "My family will be home soon and we will get it all worked out as soon as my father gets here, you'll see."

"Your father?" I jumped back, in shock, "I thought you lived here alone, and your father… well, he must have powers then? What if he doesn't like me and zaps me or something?"

Laughing uncontrollably, Charlie moved closer and ran his hand over my hair, "You watch too many movies," he snickered at me.

Chapter Four

It took Charlie only a few minutes to calm down my hysteria. He explained to me that people don't just go around zapping each other and that our whole existence was actually more natural than I might think. I began to feel more and more comfortable with Charlie as time passed. My stomach was still hostilely taken over by butterflies, but the rest of my nerves had completely settled.

Charlie was explaining to me how he and his family had never heard of any other moon beings in the area and that all of them that he knew of were in families or tribes when we heard the door opening. In walked two more of the most beautiful people I had ever seen. Charlie's father must have been in his late thirties or early forties. He had dark, silky hair and deep, sensitive eyes. He looked like a classic movie star, reminiscent of Cary Grant. The woman who walked in behind him was just as stunning. She also had dark hair, with a very warm burgundy hue to it. Her eyes were blue, like Charlie's, and just as devastatingly striking, except hers had a slight hint of grey, where Charlie's were as blue as deep body of water.

Charlie stood up to greet his family and to introduce me, but with one glance at me, his father and his sister both shot him a stunned and mortified look. *Uh oh, I shouldn't be here.*

"What have you done, Charlie?" his father sneered at him.

"Now, Nathan, calm down. There is a reasonable explanation for this" Charlie protested.

"There had better be!" the women shot back.

"You stay out of this, Gwen. She doesn't concern you." Charlie answered her with such aggression behind his eyes it startled me. This was the monster in him being exposed. I ran to his side and put my hand on his arm. I wanted to calm him. I would not allow myself to be the reason for this family to fall apart.

"It's fine, Danni, stand back." I wished that he didn't keep telling me to back off and sit down. We had barely known each other for two days now and he had bossed me around more than any other man had my whole life. I let out a large sigh and backed off.

Some time between their entrance and my jumping to Charlie's side, something changed with Nathan. His expression was much more pleasant now, but still bared the implications that he was stunned.

"How could this be, Charlie? Is it true?"

That gorgeous smile of Charlie's was back, "Yes, you can sense her then. It's true. I found her last night and I'm positive that she is", Charlie answered his father, still not paying any attention to Gwen. Gwen did not relax her posture at all. I wondered if she could sense the same thing that Nathan did and if she understood what they were talking about.

Charlie stepped back to where I was standing and put his hand on the small of my back, "Nathan, Gwen, this is Danni. Danni, this is my family." I took a step forward and reached my hand out to greet them,

"It's a pleasure to meet you", I said in the most relaxed voice I could find.

Nathan stepped forward and reached for my hand. His hand was cold to the touch, but was smooth and soft, "The pleasure's all mine", he replied, then looked to Gwen, "Please go down to the cellar and get us a bottle of wine, Gwen, we have a guest."

Charlie started to protest, "Oh, no, she's…"

But I stopped him, "No, it's fine, really." I didn't want to seem rude and I was beginning to really get thirsty anyway. I had always been allowed a little wine by my mother, and I didn't want to appear immature in front of Charlie and his family.

He did not appear to condone my decision to have a glass of wine and I found it peculiar that Charlie had become so protective of me in such a short period of time. I followed him back into the living room and joined him on the couch while Nathan stood back watching us intensely. Gwen walked into the room with an uncorked bottle of wine and set it down on the glass table, then swiftly turned around and returned to the kitchen for the wine glasses.

"So, Danni, tell me about yourself", Nathan inquired.

"I really don't know what to say", I replied softly. Charlie jumped in, finally deciding that he should take a seat after all. He sat so close to me that I could feel his arm brushing against mine, causing me to blush slightly. Gwen stayed standing behind where Nathan was seated, still silent and still glaring at me. She doesn't like me. I nervously picked up my glass and took a sip, hoping that some one else would say something to break the tension. The wine was intoxicating. I had never tasted anything like it before, but I could feel it heating first my throat, then my stomach.

"Stop!" Charlie grabbed the goblet from my hand. "She's not ready for this, she only just found out", he protectively told Nathan.

"It's okay, Charlie, really. I've had wine before. I'm not a child, you know", I protested.

"Yes, I'm sure you have, but I expect that you aren't quite ready for your first glass of blood, and to be honest I don't think you are remotely close to being prepared for a step like that. What, have you known you are a moon child for an hour now and you are already diving into the blood?"

He looked at me hurt at first, but when he saw the painstaking shock I was in, his protective side took the forefront.

"Moon beings found long ago that a blood supplement boosts their powers, hence the vampire fables," Charlie explained taking the glass out of my hand and setting it onto the glass table.

"My apologies", Nathan said now looking solely at Charlie while he spoke to me, "I was not aware that you were so new to this life. Please, tell me then, how has it been kept from you for so long?"

Of course I knew that my mother could not possibly have known that I was a moon child. But then I realized that if Ella did not know what I was, then Daniel must have. Daniel was the only answer.

"I think that my father was the one", I began, "but he has been dead now for years." "Interesting, very interesting indeed", Nathan remarked, still not looking at me. It was odd the way his eyes were burning at Charlie, but for the moment, I was glad that they were not on me. It was uncomfortable enough to sit there with Gwen looking at me as if I had just killed her puppy.

"I have to get Danni home", Charlie stated while grabbing my arm and rising suddenly. I must have missed something that transpired at that moment. Whatever his reason, I was grateful to Charlie for putting an end to the evening. I had had enough excitement to last me a lifetime and I was ready to be home where all was normal, or where I felt most normal anyhow.

Charlie did not wait for any goodbyes or formalities. By the time I had even registered what had just happened I was already in his car and driving back up his long and spiraled driveway.

"I'm so sorry about that, Danni. I had no idea that they were going to react that way."

"What exactly did you think was going to happen tonight?" I asked.

"I thought that Nathan would be more help, or that they would be as excited to meet you as I was. I thought that they were going to at least be accepting."

"They were fine" I lied.

"Yea, fine if you have a death wish. I
don't know what Nathan was getting at, but
whatever it was, I'm going to find out. Which
way?" I gave him turn-by-turn directions to my
house, but other than that we were both silent.

He pulled into my driveway and turned to
me, "Danni, I need to see you again."

"Sure", I answered.

"When?" he asked, "Tomorrow?"

I nodded.

"I'll be here at nine in the morning, and
Danni, don't worry, I'll take care of
everything." I was only half awake at this
point and nodded again, speechless. Charlie
kissed me on the forehead and walked around the
car to let me out, "Tomorrow, nine, don't
forget", he instructed.

I just nodded again and walked to my door.

When I walked into my house my mom was
waiting for me, "Fun date?" she asked.

"Uh huh" was all I could force out.

"Are you going to see him again?" she interrogated.

"Tomorrow, nine" I informed her.

She smiled, "Get some rest than, you're going to need it."

Was she ever right! Ella had no idea what kind of night I just had and what kind of day I could only guess that I was in for.

"Goodnight Mom" I sighed on my way up the stairs. "Goodnight Danni, sweet dreams", she called.

As tired as I was, getting to bed that night proved to be very difficult. My mind was having a hard time grasping everything that had happened, all in one day. I was exposed to a world that I had known to only be fantasy. I sat face to face with real people with super powers. I tasted what I could only guess to be human blood. I found out that my father was

quite possibly something called a moon being,
making me a moon child. But, then, I also
spent the entire day with Charlie and would be
seeing him again in the morning. The thought
of Charlie flooded my mind causing my heartbeat
to climb and then steadily slow until finally,
I was asleep.

Chapter Five

I was awakened at precisely 8:00am by loud music streaming from the kitchen. Ella had awoken early to make me breakfast for what she presumed was a second date with a dreamy guy and she was very cheery about it. I made my way down to the kitchen to find her with the music channel on the television blaring and Ella dancing around the kitchen singing into the spatula.

"Good morning, sunshine", I greeted Ella sarcastically.

"Good morning to you, sweetheart, I hope you're hungry", she responded in her upbeat voice. In fact, I was hungry. I was actually rather famished. I realized that I had not eaten much of a meal other than some veggies the day before, unless you count a glass of blood as a meal, which I do not. At this thought, my stomach turned slightly, but not enough to deter my attention from the plate of food that was now sitting in front of me. I ate so fast I barely even realized what I was eating.

I sat at the kitchen counter watching my mom for a couple of minutes, wondering if she had any idea about what dad was. I thought to ask her, but decided against it. If she had known, I think that Ella would have told me. She is not the type that easily keeps secrets and this would have been too large a secret for her to be able to contain.

I thought that it would be best for me to keep the information I had just learned to myself. I was still not sure that my father was a supreme being of any kind at all and even if he was, I preferred not to tarnish his image in her eyes. She had loved him more than life itself, and breaking her heart was not something that I was willing to do.

I thanked Ella for the delicious breakfast, although, truthfully I could not be sure if it was really delicious or not being that I was so hungry just about anything would have looked good to me and I did not wait long enough between bites to really savor any of the flavor. After eating, I almost always get really cold. I wondered if this were normal or if this was one of my symptoms. I made a mental note to ask Charlie about it when I saw him.

I took a quick hot shower to warm me up and stood in front of my closet for what felt like ages trying to decide what to wear. I was not sure what Charlie and I would be doing today so getting dressed was rather difficult. I decided that blue jeans were always safe so I chose my favorite pair of jeans, the ones I wore almost every day, and a plain white shirt that looked nice against my creamy skin. I noticed that my skin looked more radiant today than usual and I wondered was the cause of this change. I threw my hair up with the red chopsticks I had purchased the day before and grabbed my leather jacket just in case I got cold, as I usually do. I made another mental note to ask Charlie about my body temperature as well.

Five minutes before nine I heard my doorbell ring. Charlie was early. Fortunately, I was ready and I rushed down to the door trying to greet him before my mother had the chance. I was too late. I think that she was waiting for him to come, because she was opening the door before the doorbell was even done ringing. Ella was inviting Charlie in when I ran up and gave her a kiss on the cheek saying goodbye. I did not want to give her a chance to interview him and I was not sure what he would say to her either.

"Nice to meet you" she was saying as I was dragging Charlie by the arm to his car.

"What's the rush, Danni?" he asked.

"I'm just ready to start the day, that's all," I replied innocently. I knew by the look he was giving me, Charlie did not believe me. I decided to begin asking him questions to distract him in order to keep him from questioning me about why I didn't want him talking to my mother.

"Do you get cold after you eat and why are I always cold when everyone else is warm? Are those two related?"

"Getting cold after you eat really is not unusual, but the other thing is related, yes." He replied. Then, he continued, seeing that I was not satisfied with that answer, "You see, our powers come from an energy inside of us, when we use that energy it heats up our core temperature, this is why our bodies run naturally cold. I use my powers a lot which is why my temperature runs warmer."

I considered what he had told me and decided that it made sense. All out of questions for the moment, I asked Charlie where we were going and his faced turned grim.

"We're going back to my house. We need to talk to Nathan." I was shocked at his answer. Wasn't it just the night before that he had rushed me out of that house because of an adverse reaction his family had to me? Something significant must have taken place from the time he returned home to this morning. The thought of sitting in that living room again sent shivers down my arms. I sat speechless, unwilling to protest to his statement knowing that whatever Charlie wanted to do must have been the best option. I trusted him and he had not yet shown me a reason not to.

When we arrived at the house, Charlie stepped out of his car and walked over to my side to help me out. I was very glad that he did because I was not sure that I would be able to muster up enough courage to exit the car on my own. He took my hand and walked me through the front door that remained unlocked. When we entered the living room Nathan was sitting on the couch with a leather bound book in his lap. He set the book on the table when he saw us and stood to greet me. Whether he was human or superhuman, the man had manners.

Just as I was beginning to feel relieved at the prospect that Gwen would not be joining us, she walked into the room holding what looked to be a bottle of wine, but I could only assume was human blood. I began to wonder how the moon beings came to acquire the human blood that they so casually referred to as wine. Was it donated like the blood that could be found at a blood bank, or were innocent people drained of it so that it could be bottled and shipped around the world for moon beings to enjoy a glass at the end of a long day? I made yet another mental note to ask Charlie about the bottled blood when the opportunity presented itself.

"Hello Danni", Gwen greeted me just barely warmer than the day before.

"Please come in and make yourself at home", Nathan invited, even though I was already in and could hardly imagine feeling at home with him and Gwen there. I inched my way in, standing as close to Charlie as I could without actually touching him. He led me to a large padded leather chair and signaled for me

to sit down. I did as he wished and Charlie
pulled a chair right next to me leaving some
distance between his family and us.

Even though it was Charlie who brought me
here to speak with his father, I could tell
that he was now second-guessing his decision.

"Okay, we are here now Nathan, so let's
talk", Charlie ordered.

Nathan furrowed his eyebrows, thinking
carefully about what he would say, and began
pouring glasses of "wine" in order to buy
himself some time before saying anything. He
handed each of us a glass and began slowly;
"Danni, I am sorry for the way I, rather, we
reacted yesterday". I could not help but to
believe him as we spoke with his smooth,
confident way. "You can only imagine what a
surprise it was to us to have been presented
with a moon child, as we have always been under
the impression that we knew of every one."

I was about to tell Nathan that he was not the only one who had been surprised with these findings yesterday, but then decided that maybe it would be best to just let him talk, so I quietly nodded my head.

Nathan looked relieved to see that I looked agreeable and continued; "You see Gwen, Charlie, and even I are sort of special. If our suspicions are correct, you are special too".

If what he was saying were true, this would be the first time in my life that I have ever been told that there was anything special about me by anyone other than my mother or Izzy-Bee.

"It is not common, practically impossible for a moon being and humans to be together because typically, the moon being will not survive the relationship," Nathan explained.

I could tell that he was trying to be tactful in trying to explain the reason that I was raised without my father. I appreciated the delicate way he was trying to tell me, none-the-less.

"That being said, my two children have been considered an anomaly in the supreme being world and after Charlie was born my love and I were forced to make a decision. Either we were to be apart for the rest of our lives to keep our children safe or we could have stayed together and risked eminent danger. My love, Julie, feared for her child and chose separation, and so the children and I came here".

I felt sorry for him, as I could detect the care he had for the mother of his children, but I also wondered what this all had to do with me. Why was this man bearing his soul to me after the intense meeting we had had before. I decided that there was something funny about the temperament of this family, and not in the comical sense.

Without thinking about how I should respond I asked, "Who made you chose? Why did you have to leave?" Something inside me told me that I needed to know.

"The moon tribe ultimately became the cause of our decision. This may be hard for you to understand at the moment, but moon beings sometimes hunt the weakest of the tribe and those who are not surrounded with other tribe members tend to become the weakest by default," Nathan responded, "and something tells me that you will become familiar with the moon tribe very soon. They will want to know more about you and your family. For starters, do you have any siblings?"

"No." I answered, "Shortly after I was born, my father died. He had been a pilot and was in a plane crash".

"Did they ever find his body?" Nathan prodded.

I shook my head no and felt a sharp pain in the pit of my stomach. *Was he implying that my father could still be alive?*

"Then, I have to assume that he might have known," Nathan stated plainly as he reached to the table and picked up the book he had on his lap when Charlie and I had first arrived. "This book contains our entire history. There are some different variations of it among the tribe, but altogether the stories are consistent and portray the same messages."

Charlie's eyes blazed into my eyes and he leaned in close to my neck and whispered, "Call your mother and tell her that we are under tornado warnings and that you will be staying the night, Nathan is going to tell you our history".

I reluctantly stood up and worked my way into the kitchen in order to make my phone call in private. I could hear Charlie, Nathan and Gwen arguing in the living room but at this point I was not worried about what they were talking about. I was worried about what I was going to say to Ella. I briefly wondered if she had any idea about what Dad was. How could she not, and did that mean that she knew what I was too?

I pushed the questions in my mind aside and dialed her phone number. Although Ella was hesitant at first, I told her that I would be sleeping in Gwen's room with her and that I was perfectly safe. Ella agreed and asked that I call her again that night before going to sleep and again first thing in the morning if the weather did not clear up in time for me to go home that night. I promised her that I would call her and hung up the phone.

I stood in the kitchen for a moment, for the first time realizing how warm and traditional it felt. It shocked me that such an untraditional family would have such a traditional kitchen.

From all of the stories I had heard about mythical creatures, so far, they have stemmed from some semblance of truth. I had to laugh at the fact that I was now thinking about something as a real being that only days ago I had thought were fantasy creations made up by very artistic people. Little did I know that someone who had contact with an actual being must have begun all of the legends hundreds of years ago. Little did I know that I would one day find out that I was more than human. Or was I less than human? Disgruntled by the thought of being less human, I dragged myself back into the living room where all was quiet and the three more or less humans were all staring up at me.

"Did she say it was okay?" Charlie asked.

"Yes, but she wants me to keep calling her to check in," I warned, mostly to Gwen in case she had any thoughts of getting rid of me in my sleep.

I sat down for what was sure to be the most interesting history lesson of my life. I was about to learn where all of the myths and mysteries of the world came from. How far back or how it began, I had no idea.

Nathan started, "In the beginning of time there were only two tribes of people, those who worshipped the sun and those who worshipped the moon. The sun beings and the moon beings did not have any reason to fight as they lived during completely different times of the day. Those who worshipped the sun had 12 hours of day and those who worshipped the moon had 12 hours of night. All was equal in the world."

"The sun tribe flourished while the moon tribe became weak and famished. The sun tribe was able to grow crops and hunt by the sun, giving them greater visibility and making it easier for them to gather food. The moon tribe became disheartened as their people died of starvation, and the population began to die off. The sun tribe grew and began expanding to cover more and more of the earth's surface with villages and farms. Today you would simply call the sun tribe humans. The moon worshippers began praying to the moon during every waking hour, first for food, and finally out of desperation merely for survival. When this did not work they began sacrificing their own people. After the first sacrifice some in the village gained a little strength, and so they thought that this is what the moon wanted of them. The more they sacrificed, the more powerful the remainder of the tribe became. Power hungry, the most powerful of the tribe began killing on their own in the backwoods of the forest. Not gaining any powers from these savage killings, this behavior became short lived.

One day a child became ill and his mother took him down to the spring to bathe him and to hydrate him. Within an hour the child was well and healthier than ever before. It was then that she realized that it was the water from the spring that was making her child well. She followed the river to a bend where there was barely a trickle of water traveling. This bend was the same place that the great sacrifice rock was located above. It was she who discovered that it was not the killings that strengthened the moon tribe, but the blood which flowed into the water they were drinking that gave them power. This is why there are no longer sacrifices, so to say, but is where the tradition of blood drinking came from. Later we would find that while not as potent as moon tribe blood, sun tribe blood offered the same rejuvenating benefits.

Pleased with the moon tribe mother for putting an end to the killings, the moon sent down a star spirit to tell his people that as they had remained faithful through famine and death, they would be rewarded with beams of the moon's power. It is from these beams that the forceful energy that we possess comes from and is passed to our children through our blood. It is also because of this powerful blood that some of the moon tribe has resorted to hunting each other, in pursuit of acquiring greater amounts of the moon beam liquidities, moon tribe blood."

Overwhelmed at the implications of the story that was just told to me, I excused myself to the restroom. I stood in front of the mirror and splashed water on my face. I could hear Charlie and Nathan having a conversation in the living room but my mind was still too ablaze with new information to be able to concentrate on eavesdropping.

It was apparent that Charlie and Nathan had a pretty heated debate about what to do next and Nathan had won. Charlie looked furious, but not defeated. He stood up from his seat and walked over to the kitchen, and went in to the refrigerator.

He pulled out a bottle of water and handed it to me, "This is for you", then grabbed what was left of the bottle of moon wine with one hand and grabbed my empty hand with the other, "And this is for me. Come on". I knew that now was not the time to argue with him about whether or not he should be drinking blood so I kept my trap shut and let him guide me up the stairs.

Nathan called up to Charlie, "You know better than to do anything stupid, Charlie." Charlie continued up the stairs without even a hint of recognition that he had heard his father speak.

When we got upstairs Charlie opened the door to his room and held the door for me to enter. I walked in, and feeling exhausted plopped onto the bed.

"Oh, what a night," I said, opening the bottle of water. I took a sip and decided that now would be as good of a time as any to call my mother and tell her that I would be going to sleep shortly. I had never had to really lie to my mother about what I was up to before and just wanted to get it over with. My conversation with Ella was brief. I told her good night, she told me she loved me and reminded me to call her in the morning.

When I hung up the phone I turned to look at Charlie. He reached his hand out to me with the bottle of moon wine in it and waved his other hand to signal for me to give him the water. Apparently, the wine just was not satisfying his thirst. I could feel heat radiating off of his body and thought that this must have been the source of his unquenchable thirst.

I exchanged bottles with him and thoughtlessly raised the new bottle to my lips.

By the time I realized what I was doing, the blood had already passed through my lips, glazed over my tongue and was warming my throat and my stomach.

"What a night," I repeated myself and took another swig, polishing off the bottle. Charlie got up off of the floor where he was seated and sat on the bed next to me, handing the water bottle back to me. It occurred to me what an intimate act sharing a bottle of water had become.

Charlie and I sat silently drinking from the bottle and handing it back and forth when he finally said, "What are we going to do? Nathan is planning on calling the moon tribe tomorrow to tell them about you".

I was not particularly happy about having to deal with any more nonhumans, let alone a tribe of them, which I imagined consisted of old decrepit men.

Charlie suddenly perked up, his brilliant blue eyes glowing as they were the first night I met him again, "I have an idea!" If we can do something to counteract to make you already a tribe member, then there is no reason for them to be concerned with you".

The idea was novel, but I still was not convinced that I was even really a moon child. Besides, I could not think of anything that we could do to suddenly make me a moon tribe member.

"We have to get married," Charlie semi-proposed. I flashed him a look that must have felt like daggers to him because he took a big drink from the bottle to work up his nerve and continued, "Not human marriage, Danni, a moon tribe binding. If we are bound together, then you are a part of my family, you will belong to my tribe. If we can be bound together before the tribe arrives, they cannot separate us, get it?"

I did understand what he was saying, but it did not by any means seem like the most logical decision to make. Having only met two days ago, I could not see how I could possibly bind myself to this man, let alone call him my husband, being that I had never had even a real boyfriend before in my life.

"I have to think about it," I replied. I really did. I did not want to become a guinea pig for the moon tribe to do as they wished with, but I did not want to be bound to a complete stranger for the rest of my life either.

"We are meant to be together at any rate. What is the difference if we do it now, or when it might be too late? The spirit has already brought us together".

I had to admit to myself that he had a valid point, but the image of what my new life would become flashed into my mind. No more future as I knew it. Just yesterday I would have thought that anything would be better than my life and today I so dearly missed what I had. It goes to show that you never really know how wonderful your life is until everything changes.

My insides feeling warm from the blood and my head feeling fuzzy from my brain working overtime, I decided it would be best for me to lie down.

"Where am I sleeping?" I asked Charlie.

"You sleep on the bed and I will sleep on the floor. I do not want to leave you alone," he replied as he grabbed a pillow off of the bed and threw it onto the floor for himself. I was grateful that he would not be leaving me alone tonight, but I was also feeling guilty about him sleeping on a cold hard floor while I got to sleep in his massive luxurious bed.

"Charlie, don't be silly, there is plenty of room for both of us up here. Just don't try any funny business," I warned.

"Scouts honor," he jokingly replied holding up his hand in a Boy Scout signal. I decided that I liked that cocky, playful side of him and hoped that I would get to see more of it once all of the drama died down.

Chapter Six

Charlie removed his shirt, revealing his
perfectly sculpted body and his creamy skin,
and climbed into bed with me. I rolled over
onto my side with my back to him. The last
thing I needed right now was to be tempted by
him, and if he was like any other guy I had
known, I knew he would be trying his hardest to
make me give in.

"Danni?" he whispered my name, waiting for
a response. I turned around to answer him when

it hit me again. The warm sugar washed over me, making my mind much more clouded than the blood and all of the troubles in the world could have made me. I closed my eyes and took a deep breath, allowing the exhilarating scent to enter my entire system.

Charlie leaned in and kissed me. This time he was kissing me on the lips. It was a deep passionate kiss that made my lips buzz with excitement. He pulled me in to him and held me tight while he kissed me even more intensely. Charlie easily rolled me onto my back and pushed himself on top of me. He felt like he was made of top grade wood, hard and solid, finely sanded, giving him a smooth finish. Rubbing his body against mine while passionately kissing me, I could feel the last ounces of control I had left leaving me quickly. Just as I started to wish that he would push against me even harder, he did, as if he could read my mind. He grabbed my hands and put them above my head, his fingers intertwined with mine.

"Let's do it now," he whispered into my ear. I was not going disagree with anything he asked of me now. "Let's bind ourselves," he continued. I have to admit that I had thought he was talking about something completely different, but still, with him on top of me, breathing his warm sugar breath all over me, I did not have a chance in hell to argue with anything that he said.

"Yes," is all I had the capacity to moan.

"Just repeat what I say," he told me, breathing hard in my ear. "I bind my soul to you," Charlie heavily proclaimed with his hand weaved back into mine. "Now you," he instructed me.

"I bind my soul to you," I repeated, trying to catch my breath. Charlie kissed me hard and pushed his body against mine even harder. Suddenly, I could feel my hand

burning. I opened my eyes and looked up to see
a silver light shining around our hands. The
light disappeared and I could see a black
tattoo, seamlessly traveling from his hand to
mine. I moaned in pleasure and released all of
my worries as our bodies molded perfectly into
each other.

When I opened my eyes the next morning, I
was not sure at first where I was, briefly
forgetting the night before. Everything came
back to me when I saw Charlie at the end of the
bed getting dressed. He flashed me a devilish
smile, exposing his perfect white teeth.

"Good morning, my wife;" he greeted me,
"You look even more beautiful today than you
did last night". At the mention of last night,
my cheeks became warm and I could tell that I
was blushing. Charlie jumped onto the bed,
playfully, and gave me a quick kiss on the
neck. "Don't forget to call your mom," he
reminded me.

"Good morning. What time is it?" I asked him, finally pulling myself together.

"Ten o'clock and we have a lot to do today," Charlie answered energetically.

Running the evening before through my mind, I was a little embarrassed, until I remembered the whole binding incident.

"How are we going to explain this to everyone?" I asked, lifting my hand and exposing my new tattoo, now panicking and fully awake.

"We'll just tell them the truth," he gave me a naughty half smirk.

"We are going to tell them that we are moon tribe and that we performed a ceremony, like human marriage, binding our souls together and that these tattoos magically appeared?" I asked.

"No, we will tell them that we had too much to drink and got matching tattoos", he laughed. I had to laugh at him. His confidence was very attractive, but his wit was becoming equally appealing.

"That is the most twisted version of the truth I have ever heard," I snorted back.

"No, my dear, the most twisted version of the truth, in this case, is actually the truth," he shot back.

"Your version it is, then," I agreed.

"Go ahead and shower, I grabbed some of Gwen's clothes for you to wear," he told me.

"That is very sweet, but something tells me that she will not be happy about me wearing her things," I answered, genuinely concerned.

"Well, she will have to learn to share; you are family now. Besides, she will be asleep until dusk anyhow," Charlie reassured me.

I got out of bed, wrapping the bed sheet around me protectively to cover myself up, even though I knew that he had already seen me the way I was, hair a mess, face unwashed and all. There was a bathroom attached to Charlie's room and I was grateful for that. Even though I knew that his family was asleep, I did not want to risk the chance of running into them in the hallway looking the way I did.

He had everything set out in the bathroom for me, a brand new toothbrush, towels, and a hairbrush, even what looked to be Gwen's makeup bag. The thought of using Gwen's things scared me a little, but I would have rather dealt with Gwen's wrath than letting Charlie see me looking so terrible.

The shower was amazingly refreshing. I could not tear my eyes away from the fresh tattoo on my hand as I washed myself. It wrapped from the front of the outside of my wrist, around the back of my hand to the center of my thumb and pointer finger. This would not be something that I would be able to hide.

After my shower, I got ready and called Ella while still in the bathroom. I was much more comfortable speaking with her when Charlie was not sitting right next to me. How was I going to explain my tattoo to her? Oddly, Ella sounded relaxed when I spoke with her. I was expecting her to be upset that I had spent the night at the house of a new guy, even though his family was there, but she did not seem to mind at all. Huh, maybe this is what being an adult is like. I suppose she was just preparing herself for me leaving for college soon. I wondered if that was going to happen now, or if everything in my life had to change.

I remembered Izzy, and wondered how I was going to tell her about Charlie and me. She was going to flip her lid when she found out that he and we had spent the night together and were an item now. I had decided that I surely was not going to be telling anyone any more than that. Something told me that trying to explain a soul binding to her would be impossible, and saying that we were just dating was the safest route.

When I walked out of the bathroom, Charlie grabbed my arm and pulled me into him, giving me a deep and sensual kiss. There it was, his intoxicating power over me; my mouth was watering as he pulled away.

"We made the right choice, I can feel it," he said. I was glad that he was so sure, because I was not. I didn't even know for sure what the whole binding thing meant. All I knew is that we had made a promise to each other and when we did something magical happened and marked us for it.

I followed Charlie down to the kitchen where he poured us each a bowl of cereal and cut bananas into them.

"We are going to need all of the energy we can get today," he said.

"What's the plan?" I asked, honestly curious.

"First, we are going to talk to your mom, while she is still awake and Nathan is still asleep. Then, we are going to come back here and show my family what has happened between us," Charlie spoke confidently. I wished that I felt as secure as he acted.

On our way to my house, I began to wonder how much, if anything my mother knew, how she was going to react and how much Charlie was going to tell her about us and about me. We pulled into the driveway sooner than I expected or was ready for, feeling as if we had just left Charlie's house. I walked in the door and Ella was sitting in the living room drinking a cup of tea.

"Hello honey;" she greeted me warmly, "So nice to see you again, Charlie," she reached out to shake Charlie's hand as she welcomed him. She looked closely at his hand and her eyes darted immediately to mine, as if she had already expected to see my matching mark. "I see that we have a lot to talk about." She spoke slowly, "Welcome to the family Charlie".

I was stunned at what I was hearing, but Charlie did not seem surprised at all.

"Thank you," he said in a self-assured tone.

Chapter Seven

The three of us sat down in my living room, which was drastically different from Charlie's upscale and enormous house. My mother poured Charlie and I each a glass of tea and offered us cookies. Charlie politely accepted, while I sat, staring at her, obviously shocked. I could not believe how normal she was behaving at such an abnormal time.

"You must have a lot of questions, Danni, so let me just explain first and if there is anything that I miss, you will have to let me know," my mother said. So she began, "Your father and I were deeply in love and had no idea that something like this could happen. We tried to live a normal life for as long as we could. He became a pilot and worked during the nights so that he could sleep all day.

"Then, one day, we found out that we were going to be having a baby. Naturally, we were both very excited, but also nervous because we had never heard of such a thing occurring.

"After a little bit of research, Dan, Danni's father, found out about you Charlie, and your sister. At first he was ecstatic to hear of your existence, until we learned of your family being separated in fear of being hunted. We knew then that we would have to hide our relationship and Danni from the world for as long as possible. Dan faked his death and vowed to never come near us again so that Danni may have a chance to live a normal life. He feared that once the moon tribe learned about our baby they might…" her words trailed off, with a look of pain and sadness, she continues, "we didn't know what they might do to you".

"Mom, what are you saying?" I cried, "You knew this whole time? You knew this whole time and you didn't tell me?" I was almost screaming, but I was horrified.

"Danni, this was our way of trying to save you. I can see that you are trying your own way now," she declared, gesturing to my hand with the binding mark on it. I couldn't believe how much about this she already knew.

"If we stay together, when we stay together," Charlie corrected himself, "she will be protected".

"I want you to find your father, Danni. Daniel Knight. He might be able to help you,"

Ella instructed me. I was shocked. Who the hell was Daniel Knight? I had been told that our last name was O'Day my whole life, and now just like that, hey your dad's not human and his last name is Knight. Have a great life, or non-life. It was all just a little too twilight zonish for me.

"So, you are telling me that my name is Daniella Knight?" I asked, still in utter disbelief.

"Actually, you should know, it's technically Daniella Law now," Charlie nudged me and smiled at the irony that we were in fact technically married and I did not even know my last name, past or present. *What a mess I am.*

"What I am telling you is that you both probably have very little time," Ella said. I followed her eyes to a set of luggage in front of my bedroom door.

"I think that this is the only way, you two better get going," Ella tried to explain.

Hot tears started burning in my eyes and
spilled down my cheeks. A huge lump in my
throat prevented me from speaking, which was
okay, because I did not know what to say
anyways. Charlie picked up my bags and carried
them to the door where my mother was now
standing, holding the door open for us to
leave.

"I love you, Danni. Take care of
yourself. I will see you again soon. I just
know it," Ella sobbed. "I love you too, mom,"
I cried, as the two of us embraced.

My body shivered on our way back to
Charlie's house. I was being bounced back and
forth from home to his house for the last two
days and now I had no home at all and barely a
family to speak of. I longed for the time when
my biggest concern was having to live on campus
at school in a couple of months, or when I
didn't want to have to figure out what to wear
to next weekend's party with Charlie's friends.

The party I knew now that I would definitely
not have to attend.

I started to think about Izzy, my best
friend. How would she feel if I never were
able to speak to her again? How was Ella going
to explain my disappearance? It was then that
I realized that this was not the first time my
mother had to let someone she loved go and do
this. This was not the first time my mother
lost someone because of this stupid tribe.

By the time we got back to the house it
was already dark and Charlie and I both knew
that his family would be awake. Having already
had an emotionally draining day, and week, I
barely had the energy to get out of the car and
I could tell that Charlie was feeling the same
way because we both sat, silently for a while.

Charlie took a deep breath and exhaled
loudly, "Okay, kid, should we do it?" I nodded
and stepped out of the car.

We were expecting to see Nathan and Gwen
waiting for us. We were correct in our
assumption. What we were not aware of was that
there would be five other people waiting with
them. All five of the newcomers were quiet
attractive. There was a woman who looked to be
in her late thirties with short blonde hair,
fair skin and sparkling green eyes. A man who
I would guess to be only a couple of years
older than Charlie, but equally as handsome,
was also present. He had dark brown hair and
dark green eyes. Two of the men looked to be
twins, with red hair and hazel eyes. The fifth
man seemed the oldest. He had slicked back
blonde hair and blue eyes that cut through you.
I thought that it was possible that these
people could be relatives of Charlie. It was a
reasonable guess, as I did not think that
people this attractive could not be related.
I, of course, was wrong.

The man with the blonde hair spoke first; "Please, come in". Charlie took my hand and guided me down into his living room. His not letting go of my hand was my first clue that these people were not family.

"I am Isaiah, a member of the moon tribe counsel," the man continued. This was my second clue that these people were not family. This was also all the evidence I needed to know that Nathan was not going to help us. Isaiah introduced the rest of the tribe to us. The woman was Elena, the twins were Brannon and Keenan and the man with the dark green eyes was Colin.

"Pleasure," Charlie replied politely to the introductions, even though his facial expression told us all that it was anything but a pleasure to be meeting the counsel.

"I understand that we may have a bit of a situation here," Elena spoke, looking directly at me.

"Nothing we can't handle ourselves," Charlie replied boldly. Elena smirked at his comment, making it apparent that she did not care what Charlie thought he was handling.

"I see the way you have been handling it, and I think that you are in over your head," Isaiah told Charlie, nodding his head to our hands and drawing attention to our tattoos.

"What have you done?" Nathan screamed, horrified, "I told you not to do anything! I told you that I would handle it! What have you done?"

"I did what I had to do," Charlie told him, calmly.

"We will, of course, have to take them both now," Isaiah informed us, "We cannot separate them now that they are bound".

"No, you must," Nathan begged, "Please do not take my son".

"Maybe there is another way," Colin started, in a surprisingly appealing Irish accent.

"There is no other way, if they are bound we will not separate them," Isaiah declared.

At that moment, I saw Nathan grab something sharp and silver and hurl it at me. Before I even had a chance to react, Charlie flung himself in front of me, taking what turned out to be a knife in his chest.

"No!" Nathan cried. I kneeled down next to Charlie who was now bleeding heavily from his chest. He looked up at me with his intense blue eyes, touched my face softly with his hand as he lay on the cold gray floor bleeding to death.

Chapter Eight

I could feel heat throbbing through my body. My head was now feeling light and my pulse was slowing to a dangerously low speed. Everything in the room started to blur together. Charlie's grip on me was becoming weaker and weaker by the moment. The heat was now burning and the pain was becoming unbearable. I dug my nails into Charlie's arm as he kept me pinned close to him. I closed my eyes, looking for some relief, as Charlie pulled me closer to him. The scent of the blood pouring out of his chest was overbearing. We lay in his a puddle of his blood, indifferent to the chaos surrounding us. Charlie's grip fell from me and his eyes closed. Charlie was gone.

I lay on top of his body, his cold, pulse less body. I did not want to move. I did not want to leave Charlie's side, just as he had not left mine until his dying breath. I could hear Nathan screaming in the background. Nathan, who had just killed his only son. Nathan, who had just killed my Charlie. My rage began to climb and I stood, my clothes, face and hair now covered in blood. My eyes locked onto to Nathan and I started towards him.

"You killed him," I accused. The palms of my hands became enflamed by my anger. I stormed towards Nathan and shoved him as hard as I could. Just as before, with Charlie, I burned a hole into Nathan's shirt. This time,

I was not caught off guard and this time I did not care if I hurt him. The heat from my palms increased and I shoved Nathan again, this time smelling burnt flesh as he backed up against the wall.

"You killed Charlie!" I screamed. I shoved Nathan with my now burning hands as hard as I could. Nathan flew back against the wall and burst into flames. Nathan was no more than a pile of ashes on the floor within seconds. I had not meant to kill him; I had only wanted to hurt him. I had no idea that I could burn someone alive by simply putting my hands on them. I turned to face the horrified group in front of me. Gwen, who I had hated before, but now felt sad for, was kneeled on the floor next to Charlie sobbing. The rest of the group looked on soberly.

Colin moved next to me and grabbed my arm. I tried to pull away, but he was too strong and his grip was too tight. Even with my new strength, Colin was much stronger than me. He

pulled me towards the front door and I stopped

fighting him. Colin was pulling me outside,

and no matter what kind of punishment he had in

store for me, I was glad to be out of that

house.

"Get in the car," he ordered me. Colin

walked swiftly over to a black sports car and

got into the driver's seat. He turned on the

car and shouted at me, "Get in now!" I

followed his order and got into the car.

Chapter Nine

I was thankful that Colin was rushing me
away from the horrific scene that just took
place. Although I wasn't sure of where we were
going, being anywhere except for Charlie's
home, where he now laid cold and dead in a
puddle of his own blood, offered momentary
relief. The terrifying thought occurred to me
that the people we left behind might be
drinking his blood as we speak. I suddenly
felt very guilty for leaving Gwen there to fend

for herself. I hadn't particularly liked her, but I had no idea what would become of her now that her family was dead and I did not want to be responsible for any harm that could come her way.

It did not seem to me that the moon tribe members who were at the Law household had any contempt against the family, so I was fairly certain that Gwen would be fine. It was me that they wanted, after all, and now, in a way, they had me.

At this thought I looked to Colin who was driving at a speed that was probably not safe. He wore a hard expression on his face and seemingly was deep in thought. He must have felt my eyes on him because he glanced at me from the corner of his eyes. His expression softened, but he remained silent.

I mustered up the courage to ask Colin where we were going, except when I opened my mouth to talk an odd squeak came out rather than words.

I cleared my throat and tried again, this time with a little more confidence, "Where are you taking me?"

Colin, very forwardly, answered me, "I've been thinking about it, and I can't drive around with you forever and I can't quite keep you now, can I? I couldn't have just left you there after everything that happened. What I have really decided is that it is not for me to decide, so I am taking you to my friend Casey's house where I believe that you will be safe for the time being, until you decide what you'd like to do next."

This was the first time that anyone had ever really told me that what would happen with my life would be my decision. While I fought and struggled against every decision that had been made for me thus far, I was now feeling abandoned and overwhelmed at the prospect of not being able to blame anyone for the wrong turns I would surely be taking down the road other than myself.

I was really expecting Colin to be more forceful if not more than the other moon beings that I had met as of late, but he genuinely did not seem interested in ordering me about. I thought that he was a dutiful man. His current self appointed duty was to get me to his friend's house safely, and rather quickly as it turned out.

We drove further and further away from the city. I could see the dim outlines of large barns spaced far from each other only to be separated by acres of farmland. Feeling drained and defeated I began to slip into sleep. The last thing I thought about as I drifted was Charlie's face.

Chapter Ten

I could hear waves crashing around me as beads of what felt like light warmed my skin. I laid still with my eyes closed absorbing the warm calm that was cast over me. Unaware of my whereabouts or surroundings, I slowly opened my eyes to what I expected to be a sunny beach. I was, in fact engulfed in light, but it was white and crisp, as opposed to the warm yellow shine from the sun. From where I lay I could see ocean waves crashing against each other, but rather than reaching a beach shore, waves were being pulled upwards towards the floating mass I was on. It was as if the waves were being pulled towards the sky by an unseen force.

I suddenly became aware of a warm body lying next to me, the back of their hand resting motionlessly against the back of mine. This person felt familiar and yet strange at the same time.

He moved the palm of his hand to align with mine and intertwined his finger, "Hello, Danni."

I tightened my hold onto his hand and turned my face towards him, "Charlie," I uttered breathlessly.

He wrapped his arm around me and pulled me to him. He was warm, the same temperature as the beams of light that were glowing on our skin. I wondered if every encounter I had had

with him after our initial meeting had been a
dream. It occurred to me that it was possible
that all of the supernatural events of my short
lived relationship with Charlie could have been
simply a dream, possibly even a reoccurring
dream.

If this is all a dream, I decided, I will
enjoy this pleasant moment of it. I will enjoy
this dream where this beautiful boy is
showering me with affection and we are not to
be disturbed by any obstacle other than my
waking hour.

I grabbed a handful of the glittering gray
sand that we were sprawled out on. I watched
it as it ran through my fingers and fell back
to the ground. I thought about how this sand
would look so beautiful in an hour glass, and
here was what looked to be an entire world made
of nothing but this sparkling grainy surface.

I had lucid dreams before, where I was
aware that I was dreaming and ultimately was

able to control the actions of dream me. To me, this was no different. If the past couple of days were dreams as well, that would make sense and fall into my pattern of lucid dreaming. Charlie and his moon tribe were more likely conjured up by my subconscious, than the likeliness that they were real.

Because I am dreaming, I will make the most of it, I thought. I rolled on top of Charlie and pressed my lips firmly against his. He kissed me back. He felt the same as he had in my other memories of him, but something was different this time. Something was missing.

I rested my head on his chest and wracked my mind on what made this Charlie different from my other Charlie. My memories traveled from one feature of his to the next; his hair, his eyes, his nose, his mouth, his skin… it finally occurred to me.

I could not smell him. Charlie had a very distinctive, intoxicating smell, but now he did not. This was not my Charlie. Everything else about him was the same, but I knew that this could not be my Charlie because my Charlie could warm my blood with a mere hint of his invigorating aroma.

I popped up, straddling him, "You're not real," I told him disappointedly.

"I am," he replied.

"But you're dead," I rebutted.

"I am," he repeated himself.

"Is this a dream?" I asked him.

"You're in a dream state," he answered cryptically.

I stood up and walked down the sandy beach of a planet, half expecting the terrain or the view to change, but it did not. Miles and miles of endless beach lay before me, hanging midair over an infinite ocean of crashing waves.

Charlie jogged to catch up with me and slowed to my pace when he reached me.

He took my hand in his, "We don't have much time. I'm not sure how long I will be able to hold on, and when I am gone, I don't know if I will be able to come back here or not."

"Do not worry, I will dream of you again," I promised him.

"I hope that is true, but that will not change my ability to be with you again, it will only be a dream. You are in a dream state, but make no mistake, I am real, and in some capacity, you are here with me."

I wanted to believe him more than anything. How wonderful it would be to be able to stay here with him.

"If this is real, then I will stay here with you," I told him.

"I wish that you could, but you will have to rejoin your body, and I will have to…" his

words trailed off at his unfinished thought.
This was it then, my final moments with
Charlie.

I looked him intently in the eyes and did
what I imagined he would want as his final
meeting with me. I moved closer to him,
putting my hand on his chest. A pained smile
appeared on his face as he reached placed his
hand over mine, covering his heart, but
stopping me from running my hand over his
chest.

This is not what he wanted, I realized.
If I were to be perfectly honest with myself,
this is not what I whole-heartedly wanted
either. More than anything, I wanted him to be
okay, but I yearned something more significant
in a final goodbye from someone who for all
intents and purposes was my deceased husband.

"Widowed at 18 and only one night spent
with a man," I joked.

"At least you waited until you were married," he countered.

"I would have let you have the milk without buying the cow, you sucker," I teased, knowing darn well that this was not really true, he knew it wasn't as well.

"In some parts of the world they worship cows, and in this case I intended to do the same," he reached for my hand, standing in front of me.

"Are you calling me fat or just saying I'm a cow?" I continued trying to ease the tension.

"I'm calling you a cow," he prodded and then pulled me in for a kiss.

So much of my time with Charlie had been spent kissing that I realized I had barely even gotten to know him, and yet I still knew that I loved him and I felt like I was sincerely connected to him in a spiritual sense.

"Damn it, Danni, you are so distracting, I can't even get to what I came here to tell you."

"I thought that you came here to tell me goodbye."

"I came here to warn you, to try to protect you. I came here to give you what you needed so that you could move on. I came here for you, and least of all, I came here to say goodbye."

"Then tell me what you need to, but do not say goodbye. I cannot bare any more of the pain of losing you."

I saw a familiar uneasy look in Charlie's eyes that made me forget where we were and what we were doing. All I wanted at that moment was to make him feel better. Coincidentally, his pain came from wanting to do the same for me.

I noticed a familiar voice calling my name from a distance. As far as I knew, Charlie and I were the only ones on this foreign land. I squinted my eyes in concentration trying to make out who the voice belonged to, searching around us for another person. I saw no one.

"What are you looking for?" Charlie asked me.

"I'm trying to see who is calling my name, it's getting clearer, but I don't see anyone" it finally hit me, "Oh, it's Colin, but I don't see him anywhere."

A look of panic took over Charlie's face, "We're running out of time and I didn't even get to tell you!"

"Tell me what Charlie?"

"I love you, Danni, and I figured it out, I know what's so special about you."

"I love you too, and you already told me, I know all about it, don't worry."

"No, you don't understand, Danni, you're a source…"

Chapter Eleven

I felt a tugging at my shoulder as Colin
called my name over and over again. I put my
hand on my seat and felt the leather interior
of what I presumed to be Colin's car, where I
had fallen asleep. I kept my eyes closed for a
moment, absorbing the dream, or non-dream, that
I had just experienced. I knew that if I
opened my eyes I would have to begin dealing
with the mess of a life that was now my
reality.

I realized that the car was not moving so I finally opened my eyes to see where we were. We were pulled up on the side of a red gravel road. There was a field of wildflowers to one side and a large barn shaped house to the other, overlooking a lake. The barn was white with red beams. It looked as if it was right out of a children's book version of a farm. I did not see any animals surrounding this barn, except for the wild birds that habituated the area.

Outside of the barn, a bright red motorcycle and a red Jeep were parked. Whoever lived here evidentially liked motorized toys. The motorcycle was sparkling clean while the Jeep was covered in mud up to its roof line. It was hard to tell what shade of red the SUV was because of the vast amount of dirt which covered it. Whenever you see a vehicle covered in dried mud, as this one was, in Minnesota, you assumed that the driver had recently enjoyed some off road driving.

Seeing that I was now awake and semi-alert, Colin opened his car door and stood up. As he stretched his arms over his head, his shirt lifted a touch, revealing his perfectly sculpted stomach and a small trail of hair that traveled up to his belly button. He glanced over at me, and sure that I had been caught looking, I looked out of my car window in the opposite direction.

He poked his head back into the car, still standing, "You getting out, or do you plan to sit in the car all day?" It would have been preferable to stay in the car, but I knew that this was not really an option.

Disgruntled, I got out of the car, feeling refreshed for the first time in days. I did not think that I was asleep for more than an hour or so, but for however long I was out, it energized me. The fresh air smelled clean and the breeze coming off of the lake relaxed me further as I stretched my arms, mimicking Colin's earlier movements, except I self consciously pulled down my shirt to make sure that I did not expose any skin as I raised my hands towards the sky.

Colin stood looking at the barn for a little bit, then turned and looked at me. Without saying anything he began walking towards the structure, and I took this as my cue to follow him. When we reached the door he knocked once, waited a second, knocked two more times, another second and then five times.

The door opened to reveal a beautiful girl who looked to be in her mid twenties. Her sandy blonde hair reached her waist and her eyelashes which framed large light blue eyes almost reached her eyebrows, they were so long and full. Unaffected by our arrival, she left the door open and turned around and walked in.

Colin took this as an invitation and followed her in, I in turn, followed him.

"Do you guys want something to drink?" she asked, reaching into the refrigerator.

"Waters, please," Colin replied for the both of us, "Casey, this is Danni. Danni, Casey," he briefly introduced us.

"Welcome," she glanced at me, completely unaffected by my wild appearance.

"Thank you," I timidly replied. I began taking in the beauty of my surroundings.

The entire structure was one level. The ceilings must have been at least 20 feet high, with beams exposed throughout. The floors were a white oak driftwood, slightly weathered and gray toned. The structure overlooked a lake and the entire wall facing the water was windowed with sliding glass doors all the way across. The doors were opened and the entire barn home was filled with a flow of fresh lake air. The kitchen was simple, with bottom cabinets matching the floors and floating shelves that held dishes on top. Large flour sack couches graced the designated living area, adorned with large fluffy fleece blankets that looked absurdly inviting.

I excused myself to the restroom, where I stood staring at myself in the mirror, still covered in Charlie's blood, now dark and dry. I heard a light knock on the door. I opened it to find a pile of clean clothes and a washcloth, neatly placed in a pile for me by Casey.

When I walked out of the bathroom, now clean, Casey handed me a glass of water and I sat down on the couch, pulling the fleece blanket into my lap without even thinking about it. I felt at home here.

The breeze picked up and carried a chill into the house. Casey looked to the doors and they all slammed shut.

"Well, you might as well tell me what you two are into, because I just tried to shut one door and we got all five." Amazing. Casey had shut the doors without even touching them. Something had gone wrong though, very similar to the glitches that Charlie had experienced with me.

At the thought of Charlie a lump grew in my throat and I tried to swallow it down before it had a chance to rise behind my eyes and release as tears.

"I'm a source," I spit out, not even knowing what exactly I was saying, but merely repeating the last thing I had ever heard Charlie say. Colin and Casey looked at me, stunned I think, at first.

Casey smiled, "You're finally involved in something interesting, Colin." Colin scowled at her remark, not quite sure of what to make of my statement, or Casey's response at that.

"Do you even know what you're claiming?" he asked me.

"No, I only know because Charlie told me when we were on our way here," I explained.

"Charlie told you when?" he asked, definitely stunned this time.

"On our way here, when I was sleeping, Charlie came to me and told me that I am a source. He seemed to think that it was important that I know, so I am assuming that it is something that you should know too as it seems that you have put yourself in the position to help me", I told him.

Colin looked at me as if I had lost my mind, and I was wondering if telling him about seeing Charlie and what he had told me was a good idea after all. I did not want to lose the only allies I had left in this world.

"I'm assuming that this Charlie is dead," Casey started, "which is why he came to you in your sleep."

"That's just your opinion, Casey, it's much more likely that she had a dream than her dead husband actually coming to her in her sleep," Colin scolded her.

"Well, you know what they say about opinions. They are just like A-holes and everybody has one," she shot back.

"Yes," Colin replied, "but some are dirtier than others."

Their argument had taken a funny turn and I couldn't help but to start laughing at this point. *Did Colin just call Casey a dirty A-hole?* Casey looked at me and started to laugh too. Clearly, she was not nearly as serious a character as Colin.

Colin finally just shrugged us off, "I guess we'll work this out tomorrow, for now I need to sleep."

Chapter Twelve

Casey woke me up bright and early while Colin was still fast asleep.

"Remember yesterday when I tried to close the door and I accidentally closed all five?" she asked me.

I nodded my head, remembering the sliding doors slamming shut and the surprised look on her face. Again, I remembered what was meant to be a slight scent being a strong fragrance, and what was meant to be a tingle becoming a shocking jolt with Charlie.

"I think that maybe there is something to this claim to you being a source. Colin will be hard to bring around, but if I am right, if Charlie was right, then this thing is much bigger than us. This thing is going to be epic."

I think that Casey forgot that "this thing" she was talking about was in fact just plain old me, and I was fairly certain, even after all that had happened to date, that nothing about me would ever be epic.

Casey and I each lay on a lounge chair outside, drinking coffee and talking until Colin woke up. She wanted to know all about me, what had happened, and all of the gory details. I explained to her the best that I could with the limited amount of knowledge that I had. She listened intently nodding as I told my story but barely saying a word through my entire explanation. Afterwards the two of us sat silently, enjoying the warm weather and the fresh air. For the second time since I had been there, I thought about how at home I felt.

Colin woke up visibly more cheerful than he was the day before, when I had met him and he saved me from who knows what. Casey rose and met Colin in the kitchen where she poured him a cup of coffee and they spoke quietly. I stayed put outside, enjoying the silence and the calm.

Colin called me inside and asked me to have a seat on the couch. I gladly curled up with the large blanket, nesting into the oversized sofa. I traced the tattoo on my hand with the pointer finger of my other hand, remembering my incredible night with Charlie the day before he was killed. Heavy hearted and somber, I looked to Colin to hear what was to be the next great, and I use the term great loosely, adventure in store for me.

"From everything Casey has told me," Colin said, "it seems that it is possible that you are a source. It is just so hard to believe because as far back as the moon tribe goes; there is only one legend of a human source in existence. The only other known source is the moon itself. All of the energy and all of the power our kind has comes from the moon, the only known source, but somehow, it seems possible that you could be channeling that power and are radiating it. I could not tell personally, because I have yet to use any powers in your presence, but Casey attests that you have magnified her powers and has also told me about what had happened with the young man we saw killed yesterday."

At the mention of Charlie, who was already weighing heavily on my heart, I felt a small stab of pain. Admittedly, there was something comforting about Colin that was putting me at ease, even at this tremendously difficult time.

The three people who had surrounded me in the past week with care, Charlie, Colin, and Casey, all had names that began with the letter C. I thought about how that was such an odd coincidence.

Casey continued for Colin, as he had stopped speaking at the first sign of my discomfort, "If you are a source, you might be able to restore our entire tribe. You could be what we have been waiting for. The problem is, like every other savior in the history of mankind, there are always some who would prefer the power for themselves rather than saving the entire species. To some, you will be worth more dead than alive."

I thought back to all of the people in history, who had been persecuted for doing nothing more than trying to better the world, most notably Socrates, Martin Luther King, Jr., Abraham Lincoln and Jesus. I would never imagine comparing myself to any of them, but considering how much more they had to offer the world and their willingness to sacrifice everything, including their lives to do the right thing, I no longer felt I had a choice to make. If I could really do anything to help my entire species, I would do so, no matter what the impending risks to me may be.

"Colin, if I gave you a name of a moon tribe member, do you think you would be able to locate the person?" I asked.

"As long as they are living within our system, it should be no problem at all," he answered.

"Daniel Knight, he is my father, and I am hoping he can help," I told him.

"I'll leave right away," Colin promised. "How much do you want me to tell him?" he asked.

"Everything," I responded.

Chapter Thirteen

Colin left right away in search of my father. Excitement, nervousness, and contempt all engulfed me. I was finally going to meet my father, but he had let me live all of these years without ever getting to know him and worse yet, believing that he was dead.

I pushed the thoughts of my paternal relationship out of my mind in order to concentrate on more important matters, like how I was going to survive long enough to help the moon tribe become a thriving part of this world again.

Upon first meeting Casey, I thought that she was all play and no work, but when it came down to business, I quickly learned that I was very wrong. From the moment that Colin left, she began training me, similar to how I imagined Charlie had planned to when he suggested it to me.

The first half of every day was filled with learning to harvest my powers. Her theory was that just as how the moon is the source of all of our powers and has the ability to absorb as well as exude them, I should be able to do the same.

We began with my absorbing her telekinetic energy, her ability to move things with her mind, by me moving little things, and then pushing harder, being able to sway trees, move the Jeep, and even create waves in the steady lake.

We then would practice me sharing my energy with her, which did not seem to deplete my level of energy at all. We created waves together, coming from opposite shores and crashing into each other in the center of the lake.

When we were not working on our supernatural abilities, Casey was teaching me martial arts. I was surprisingly quick at learning techniques in Brazilian jiu jitsu and Muay Thai, two very popular training areas of mixed martial arts. We spent hours grappling in the sand along the water, perfecting arm bars, choke holds, sweeps, and the like. Casey was a machine, and she was set on turning me into one too.

After looking at Casey's filthy, mud covered Jeep I finally could not take it any longer. One morning I grabbed a bucket of soapy water and made my way out to the road facing side of the barn with every intention of getting that thing clean. Before I even had a chance to get started, Casey busted me.

"What do you think you're doing?" she asked me.

"What does it look like?" I answered, "This thing is filthy."

She arched her brow, "Well, how do you plan to take care of that?" she questioned.

"I'm going to wash it," I wondered if she thought I was an idiot or something.

"And how, may I ask, do you plan to do that?" she continued.

At this point I thought that she was getting ridiculous, "I'm going to pick up the freaking wet sponge and wash the disgusting thing."

"No, you're not," she told me.

"Oh, but I think I am," I shot back. I really did not think that I could handle looking at that filth for another day.

"You can wash the truck," she instructed me, "but if I see you touch the sponge or the Jeep, you're running six miles tomorrow, do you understand?" I did, and this became another aspect of my training; household chores, starting with the washing of the truck would be done by telekinesis. Truthfully, once I got the hang of it, and stopped breaking dishes when trying to wash them, this became my preferred method of taking care of household tasks.

We went on like this for weeks with only the occasional word from Colin letting us know that he was hot on the trail of Daniel Knight. Colin also had word as to what had happened at Charlie's house after we left. It turned out that Gwen, who I thought to be someone who I could not trust, had saved me. She had told the rest of the moon tribe members that I was not one to be worried about, and that I had not even exhibited any demonstration of power. She sold me as a scared and useless child not to be bothered with. A part of me wondered if she really felt that way, but the rest of me was just very grateful.

Finally, the call we were waiting for from Colin came, "I'm with Mr. Knight, we should meet in the city."

Chapter Fourteen

Casey and I packed up the shiny and clean Jeep. Not knowing how long we would be away from the lake house, we thought it would be best if we were prepared for a long stay. The Jeep, by the way, was a light cranberry red once it was freed of all of the grit and grime.

Colin had a condo in downtown Minneapolis where he thought it would be wise for us to meet him. Even though being secluded worked to our benefit until this point, he and Daniel decided that the convenience and the resources of the city would now be beneficial.

By this time Casey and I had become very close friends. In some ways, she reminded me of Izzy. They were both so strong willed and spontaneous. Additionally, they both seriously lacked filters in terms of expressing their thoughts or opinions and neither one of them had any trouble coming up with the most absurd ways of using inappropriate language. Fortunately, those absurd ways were also absurdly hilarious.

On the drive back to the city, I told Casey about my life before the moon tribe came into my realm. I told her about my mom, Ella, my friends, and about what my plans for the future were. More than anything, she was really interested in the experience of high school and what it was really like. She had seen a lot of movies about kids in regular schools and read some books on the subject, but this was an aspect of life that was foreign to her as she was home schooled the way most of the moon children were.

"Hey, Casey, I've been with you for a while now and, I was wondering, when do you drink blood?" During my entire stay with her, I did not see one bottle of blood or witness her take one sip of it.

"How in the world did you hear about that?" she asked. "That practice has been dead for years. Only the truly power desperate families still continue that tradition, but as a tribe, it is really discouraged."

Casey explained further that in the beginning the blood came from injured humans, later to be replaced by donations when blood banks came to be. Now, whatever supply is used by old fashioned moon tribe members who insist on following this tradition is bought on the black market from moon tribe members who become blood bank employees for the sole purpose of selling to the moon beings.

This explained a lot about Nathan to me. I had sensed something off about him, and now I was sure that any strange behavior by his children had to have been by his influence. At that, I was relieved that blood drinking was not a practice that I would have to get used to. Like any other culture, some of the more savage of traditions had been phased out. Unfortunately, the hunger for power has not died down in any culture and neither have the rapid declination of morals and the value of life.

We drove for almost four hours, talking nonstop, before we reached downtown Minneapolis. When we reached the city, the streets were unusually full. I had never seen Minneapolis so busy, crowded like the Las Vegas strip on New Years Eve. I didn't remember the city ever being so highly populated. Casey did not notice anything out of the norm as she was not accustomed to the city anyhow. She assumed that the city was always this jam packed and remarked about that being just another reason why she preferred living where she did.

We pulled up to a tall brick building, each unit distinguishable from the exterior by the large balconies attached.

We parked the car and walked up to the building entry.

"Are people out here always like this?" she asked me. Unsure of what she meant, I glanced around us. While no one was looking directly at us, I got the distinct feeling that we were being watched, and not by just one person, but possibly many.

Without using her hands to push the buttons, Casey dialed up to Colin's unit. Even though I had spent day after day watching her use her telekinesis, I still got a kick out of even the most simple of acts, such as dialing numbers with her mind. The funny thing is that when I am near her, I am able to do so too. Using powers, however talented I may have gotten at it, still felt foreign and unnatural to me. I had already decided that it would probably take me long time to get used it, if I ever did.

Colin answered and we announced our arrival to him. He buzzed us into his lobby, where a uniformed guard sat at the front desk. He smiled at us and we politely said hello. The lobby was plush with marble floors, and elegant furniture, making the price point of the building obviously in the upper echelons of Minneapolis living.

We took the elevator to the thirteenth floor, where his condo was located. Neither of us said anything on the elevator trip up. I think that we were both feeling the exhaustion of the long car ride kicking in and at least I was trying to ignore the gnawing feeling in my stomach that something unexpected was afoot.

Walking down the hallway, towards Colin's door, I started thinking about what my first meeting with my father would be like. Meeting him had been an impossible dream my entire life because I was under the impression that he was no longer alive. When I did find out that he was living, meeting him was merely a theoretical idea. That idea was about to come to fruition and the nerves were kicking in.

I slowed my steps, falling a few paces behind Casey, seeing that she did not seem hurried to reach Colin's home either. What was to follow was unexpected for both of us. For me, I was to meet my father for the first time in my life and decide the direction for the rest of my life, and for her, she would learn what her part would be in the future of her entire tribe.

My heart started to race. Casey stopped in front of what was presumably Colin's door and turned back to look at me. I stopped where I was and leaned against the wall. Bent over at the waist, with my hands on my knees, I closed my eyes to try to gather myself. The enormity of the situation finally weighed upon me and I could feel the pressure physically pulling me downward. Hot tears started running down my cheeks.

Casey walked back to me and sat crossed legged on the floor next to where I was hunched.

"We are going to stay right here until you are ready, and if you don't ever get ready, then we will not go in," she said simply. Her words soothed me a bit, one less person putting pressure on me. "Whenever, if you are ever ready to do this, I will be by your side. If you decide that this is not what you want to do anymore, we will turn around and go back to my house," she reassured me. The thought of going back to her house was so appealing, but I knew that I could never bring myself to do that. I had already decided that I was going to do anything in my power, however small or great that power may be, to help people.

I took a deep breathe and stood up straight.

"Ok," I nodded, "let's go in." Casey stood up and wiped the tears from my face with her sleeve.

"You're going to be fine. *We're* going to be fine," she assured me.

Chapter Fifteen

Colin answered his door, dressed much more casually than he had been when I met him. His visit to the Law household had been a formal one, but now, within his own home he looked much more comfortable in a pair of jeans and a t-shirt. Seeing him so informal relaxed me a bit.

My eyes immediately wandered to the strange man inside. He leaned against a black baby grand piano which occupied the center of the main living area. His eyes met mine and flashed familiarity at me, but then quickly went back to the blank stare he initially had given.

My first thought was that this man could not be my father. Daniel must have been at least fifty years old by now, but this man did not look much older than thirty. None of the moon tribe I had met had looked their age, I reasoned, so why should Daniel be any different. This must be my dad.

Daniel stepped towards Casey and me as we walked in.

He first introduced himself to her, and then, very formally, he shook my hand, "It's nice to finally meet you, Daniella, you look very much like your mother."

My stomach turned at the mention of my mother. I loved my mother very much and I did not see the love or affection in my father's eyes that I was so used to receiving from my mother. I had always thought that love was something that was ingrained between parents and children, but now, for the first time, I saw first hand that this was not true. The love between my mother and me was built, earned, and shared. This man was and very much felt like a stranger. Being in his presence made me miss my mother even more than I had, and I immediately promised myself that I would go see her the moment that I knew it would be safe to.

The thought of hugging my mother choked me up, so I distracted myself by taking in my surroundings. Colin's home was unique, much like Casey's, and even Charlie's, but his was so in a different way. His finishes and materials were typical, but his furniture arrangement was anything but normal.

The black baby grand piano was the centerpiece of his design. To the left were an

open kitchen and the door leading to the
bathroom, these parts, I imagined were standard
for units in his building. To the right,
however, it looked as if the wall to what must
have previously been the bedroom had been
removed, as well as the wall to the master
bathroom. A large bed and bathtub were visible
from any point in the home. The couches were
nonexistent. Colin lived with a kitchen, a
piano, and an exposed bed and bath. Colin was
a minimalist, at most.

I considered how lovely this must be when
he is alone to enjoy the open living space and
I realized that having guests must be an alien
concept to Colin. I had to give him credit
though; he seemed very much at ease with having
us in his obviously private home.

Colin invited us to have a seat. Casey
and I rested on the edge of the bed while
Daniel sat down on the piano bench. I looked
at Daniel, expecting him to ask me how I've

been, tell me how great it is to finally meet his daughter, or some kind of personal statement, but he looked at the floor and said nothing.

I wondered how my mother could have fallen in love with such a dry, impersonal man, when she was such an outgoing and bubbly woman. I decided that the man he was today could not have been the same man who she had known. Not literally, of course, but in the sense that he must have changed dramatically over the past 18 years.

Intuitively, Colin brought us each a bottle of water and a sandwich to eat. I had not even realized how hungry I was until I had the sandwich in my hand. We had not eaten since before we left the lake house earlier in the day and all of the anticipation of meeting my father had depleted my appetite. Now that my meeting with my dad was decidedly anticlimactic, my appetite was returning.

"So, what's the plan?" I asked Colin with a mouth full of food.

"Don't talk with your mouth full, and nothing has been decided. Daniel wanted to wait until you were here before we began discussions on what your future might entail."

Reminded that this meeting was to be centered on me and my future, I shifted uncomfortably on the bed making it move so that Casey spilled the water she had been drinking on herself. She frowned at me while she wiped it up.

"Ok, I'm here, so let's talk," I declared. Daniel looked up at me for the first time since our meeting with a somber expression on his face.

"I think what's best is that Daniella comes back with me to live with the moon tribe," Daniel stated plainly.

I didn't like the way he said my name, *Daniella*. No one who knew me at all called me that, as far as I was concerned my name was just Danni. That alone reminded me that this man did not know me at all and that I knew living with him and a bunch of strangers would be the last of the options I would chose.

"Well, that's probably not going to happen," I said, "So, what else have you got?"

"You're a child," he told me, "How could you possibly know what to do in such an important situation like this one?"

What a jerk! In the past few days I had been told that I was less than human, more than human, supernatural, an anomaly, and many other things, but since the beginning of this entire ordeal, he was the first person to actually tell me that I am a child and discount my opinion as if it carries no weight.

"I am a married woman and a widower. I am legally an adult and a high school graduate. Lastly and what seems to be most importantly, I am a source," I declared standing up and putting down my mostly eaten sandwich. I had to take a stand, assert myself in what I was deeming a hostile situation.

Colin and Casey stood speechless, rarely hearing me raise my voice. Granted, Colin did actually witness me kill a man within moments of meeting me, a fact that continually slipped my own mind. The entire scene of Nathan killing Charlie, and then me incinerating him played in my mind as I stood there silently looking down at Daniel, awaiting his next move.

He did not move, but casually looked up at me, "You are a spoiled child."

"It was my decision to include you in our discussion, and now I am making the decision to remove you from our process. I thought that I was asking my father for help, not this, whatever you are!" I screamed.

"You think you can just *remove* me? That is just a small example of your immaturity. I already know what you are, where you are, and who you are with. Do you think that you can just go undetected? This is not about you. This is about an entire species, an entire tribe. This is about my tribe and my life just as much as it is about yours. You think that I have not considered the fact that you are my only child? Of course I have, but my duty is to my tribe. I fulfilled my duty to you years ago. I gave you life. I gave you powers. I am the reason you breathe and you owe me everything!" he retaliated.

At that Colin moved between Daniel and me and Casey moved closer to my side. It was my choice to include my father and I was now regretting that decision more than any other I had ever made.

Colin put his hand on my shoulder, "Let's step outside for some air." I was glad that he gave me a way out. Arguing with my dad is not how I had intended on spending my night and I was becoming weary.

Colin pushed aside the curtains to reveal
a large door to his balcony. The balcony was
made of stone and had a thick ledge, guarded by
stone gargoyles. The view of the city was
breathtaking from here. The faint sound of
cars and people traveled to us as we sat
directly above the scene on the thirteenth
floor, far enough to be removed from everything
and still have an eagle eye view of it all.

I imagined Colin, during his time alone,
playing his piano with the curtains drawn open,
being inspired by the liveliness of his
surroundings.

"This is horrible," I told him. "If I had
known that having my dad around would be so bad
I would have never even considered it."

"I don't want you to think that it's
always like this, with dad's I mean," he said.
"It's just that I can't help but notice that
you first had a bad experience with Nathan and
now with your own father, and I don't want you

to think that this is what being a dad looks like. All of the best things about me come from my dad and for him from his father. Even my power has been passed down from father to son through the generations."

"You know, I don't think that I have seen you use your power even once yet. What is it?"

"Well, the simple answer is strength," he told me.

He was definitely in shape, but he did not look like a steroid pumped body builder.

"You have super human strength?" I asked him skeptically.

"So, you know how the Greek myths are based off of those from the moon tribe?"

I nodded my head, wondering where he was going with this.

"I am a direct descendant of Hercules."

"The Irish Hercules?" I could not stifle my laugh.

"And here I thought you were one of the bright ones," he teased me. "We all came from the same place, genius. Two tribes. Moon tribe. Sun tribe. One place. We don't lose our heritage just because we move locations and submerge into new cultures. We are who we are."

"And you are a Greek god," I teased him. Now that he said it, I could not help but compare him to Michelangelo's David. Even though David was a biblical figure, the statue always looked very Greek god like to me.

"To be fair, my grandfather, a few greats down the line, was," he joked back.

"So," I asked him, "if your power is inherited, then does that mean that mine is too? If so, why doesn't he just go be the almighty source himself?"

"That's why I brought you out here. There is something that I think you should know about Daniel before you pass any judgment on him."

"I'm listening."

"Dani, your father doesn't have any powers, not any more."

"Wait, how can this be? I thought that everyone in the moon tribe had something, even if they were small powers; I thought that they all had some at least. Charlie had the electricity and pheromone things, you have the strength, and Casey has telekinesis…"

"Well, we have a theory on that. You know how you can source energy, but also absorb it? We think that when you were born you instinctively absorbed all of the energy around you, except the only tribe member around you was Daniel, so you depleted his entire supply. He has been living with the tribe powerless for your entire life, not to protect him, but to protect you. Now that he knows that you are a source, he sees this as his chance to get his powers back."

I felt badly for him. I could now see why he thought that I was a spoiled brat. Here I was with what was deemed an infinite amount of power and Daniel had none because I was born. This was not a guilt that I was expecting to be confronted with.

Chapter Sixteen

The air seemed stiffer when we walked back inside. I knew that it was probably just my imagination, but it made it harder to breathe, none the less. A difficult decision was now made impossible. I knew two things; first, that I had to somehow make up for the fact that I had taken all of my father's powers at birth, and second, that I had to find a way to use these powers for good without being turned into a prisoner.

"Dad?" When I called him this, he turned to me, looking surprised. "Dad," I continued, "I'm going to help you, and find a way to help everyone, all of the moon tribe, but I need you to trust me. Can you do that? If you trust me, then we can work together."

At this, I thought that he would be pleased, but he looked more distressed now than he had even before.

"I didn't come alone," he confessed.

A part of me had already known this. Casey and I had noticed an unusual amount of people lining the streets and I had felt like I was being watched as we walked up to Colin's building earlier. Now I knew that I was right. My father had brought reinforcements. Unfortunately, these reinforcements were not for me, but rather for the moon tribe.

"What have you done?!" Colin shouted.

"How was I to know?" Daniel asked him. "How was I to know what to expect? My first duty is to the tribe."

"Your first duty should have been to your daughter, but you're just like the others, blinded by power," Colin said angrily. "Your efforts will go wasted. You're not the only one who did not know what to expect from this meeting, and I am not one to ever be unprepared."

At this Casey ran onto the balcony, her eyes darting back and forth on the street seeing the crowds of people who had come to either imprison or defend me.

"You won't be taking her," Colin swore. "She is under our protection."

"I don't have a choice," Daniel answered.

At that Colin picked up his piano and hurled it at the door to create a barricade. Casey stood in the center of the room with her arms above her head, ready to fight whoever

came our way. Daniel, had planned for this,
and within seconds of Casey and Colin taking
defensive stands threw a flare off of the
balcony, signaling our resistance.

Chapter Seventeen

Fighting exploded on the streets. What
looked like hundreds of people were now engaged
in a massive battle. Cars were flying from one
end of the road to the other, and smashing into
storefronts. Fires erupted and chaos ensued.

Daniel, a powerless man, had started this
over me, a powerful girl. My family, I was
convinced, was cursed. The front door smashed
open and people charged into the condo,
breaking Colin's large piano into small,

shattered pieces. I was in complete shock and
stood still watching the terror around me while
my friends sprung into action.

Casey swung the chandelier off of the
ceiling and onto a group that was attacking us
while Colin picked people up and flung them
like Frisbees.

I slowly took steps backwards,
unconsciously absorbing the powers of the
trespassers as I backed away, giving Colin and
Casey a distinct advantage against our
aggressors.

When I reached the balcony, I looked down
over my shoulder to see the horror of the war
below. Blood bathed the once clean
metropolitan streets. This time, on purpose, I
began absorbing powers.

I hopped onto the ledge of the balcony,
standing in between two stone gargoyles with my
back to the street. I did not want to see the
pain any longer.

With no prejudice as to whose power I was
taking, I began to absorb. I could feel the
different powers channeling through me, making
me stronger, and I continued. The more I
absorbed, the quieter the battle below me
seemed to get. The more I absorbed, the slower
the attacks into the building seemed to become.
The more I absorbed, the less I heard or saw of
the outside world.

This power, that was supposed to be a
gift, was being abused and used not to
strengthen the tribe, but to deplete it. Moon
tribe members were killing moon tribe members;
even now, in a time of civilization.

I closed my eyes and concentrated. I
concentrated on absorbing every last bit of
power within my reach. I felt an explosive
surge inside of myself and silence fell around
me.

In the end I knew that I had to make a
sacrifice. I would absorb all of power that

was turning moon tribe souls black and take the darkness with me.

I took a step backwards and opened my eyes as I fell. The sound in my mind had completely shut off. I saw Colin run in slow motion towards me, reaching over the railing trying to grab a hold of my hand. Rather than reach up at him, I spread my arms outwards and looked up at the dark starry sky, feeling the breeze travel across my body as I fell backwards towards the earth.

www.ingramcontent.com/pod-product-compliance
Lightning Source LLC
Chambersburg PA
CBHW020435180626
46812CB00003B/1253